MURDER STRIKES AT MIDNIGHT

Rooftop Garden Cozy Mysteries, Book 6

THEA CAMBERT

Summer Prescott Books Publishing

Copyright 2020 Summer Prescott Books

All Rights Reserved. No part of this publication nor any of the information herein may be quoted from, nor reproduced, in any form, including but not limited to: printing, scanning, photocopying, or any other printed, digital, or audio formats, without prior express written consent of the copyright holder.

**This book is a work of fiction. Any similarities to persons, living or dead, places of business, or situations past or present, is completely unintentional.

CHAPTER 1

"Here's to Alice! Yet again, she successfully oversaw the Blue Valley Hometown Holidays festival—and this year, there wasn't a single dead body in the giant bowl of jelly!" Owen James raised a mug of hot cocoa into the air.

It was an odd toast, but the friends gathered together in the rooftop garden above Alice Maguire's bookshop, The Paper Owl, all understood its meaning. The Christmas before, the three friends—Alice, along with Owen James and Franny Brown-Maguire—had run their first-ever race together. But the Bowl Full of Jelly 5k had turned into a nightmare when a body was found in the giant bowl of jelly.

This year's festival, however, went off without a

hitch, without a murder, without a single malfunction right down to the town's rousing annual performance of the beloved play, *A Christmas Carol*, starring Chester Lehman owner of Blue Valley Hardware, as Ebenezer Scrooge.

After taking a generous swig of Franny's signature hot cocoa (the secret was in the melted chocolate bars and swirls of marshmallow cream), Alice wiped a dot of froth from her nose with the back of her hand and smiled at her friends.

"Mark my words: I will *never* be in charge of the Hometown Holidays Festival ever again!" she announced.

"Oh, I doubt that," said Franny, shaking her head.

"Sure, you will," said Owen with a snort. "Mayor Abercrombie will put on those sad eyes of his and beg you to do it, and you'll succumb."

"Succumb?"

"Cave in."

Alice rolled her eyes. "I will do neither of those!"

"Exhibit A," said Owen, taking out a small packet and handing it to Alice.

"What's this?"

"*This* is the photographic evidence that supports my theory that you will always be in charge of every festival Blue Valley ever hosts for all time. And that's a lot."

It was true. Blue Valley was a quaint little town, snuggled into a valley deep in Tennessee's Smoky Mountains. It wasn't on any of the main roads, but happily lay just off the beaten path, surrounded by ancient, rolling green mountains. It boasted a lake and woods and a bustling Main Street. The locals knew they were the luckiest people on earth to live in Blue Valley—and the visitors who wandered far enough into the mountains and discovered the place, returned season after season for the many festivals and fairs the town put on.

Alice opened the packet to find a small stack of photos.

"You took these with your new camera? The one my parents gave you?" Alice raised a brow at Owen, who proudly smiled in return.

"Yep. Martin and I both have this model now. We're taking our cameras on our bird-watching expeditions."

It never ceased to amaze Alice that her parents seemed to have adopted Owen James. She was always surprised when he'd casually mention that he'd been baking with her mother, birdwatching with her father, even exchanging postcards with Alice's globetrotting Granny Maguire! This year on Christmas morning, when the whole family gathered at the Maguires' house over by Town Park, Bea and Martin had excitedly presented Owen with the camera, and he and Martin had rushed right outside, where they photographically captured Yellow-rumped Warblers and White-throated Sparrows in the wild—a.k.a. the Maguires' backyard.

Alice's building housed three businesses that fronted Main Street: In the middle was The Paper Owl, where Alice always stocked the latest bestsellers, the classics, and hot-off-the-presses issues of several newspapers, including the *Blue Valley Post*. On one side of the bookshop was Sourdough, Owen's bakery—famous for its decadent sin-amon rolls. On the other side was Joe's, Franny's coffee shop, which served the best coffee in town and quite possibly, in the world. The three friends were also neighbors, because they lived in the small apartments above their shops, and together, they had created the amazing rooftop garden that overlooked Main Street.

In the fall, Franny—who'd been fast friends with Alice since their middle school days—had married Alice's brother, Ben, captain of the Blue Valley police force. Ben had a cozy house by Blue Lake, and after they married, Franny and Ben spent time in both homes, because they just couldn't choose one or the other.

Alice leafed through the photos Owen had handed her, and Franny looked over her shoulder.

"Ha! There we are at the finish line of the race!" said Franny. "We're covered in jelly!"

The Bowl Full of Jelly 5k Fun Run featured a gauntlet of silly obstacles. Participants had to climb up the new-fallen-snow slippery slope, leap over eight tiny reindeer, and slog through a giant bowl full of jelly, in order to earn their medals and commemorative t-shirts.

"I was glad Barb went with sugarplum jelly this year," said Owen. "So festive."

"What even *is* a sugarplum?" asked Franny.

"Whatever the flavor, it didn't feel all that festive when I was trying to get it out of my hair," said Alice, whose curly red hair was both her crowning glory and her curse.

"There you are, Alice, opening the Mistletoe Market," said Owen, calling Alice's attention to the next photo. "See how you have your little microphone and your little holiday outfit?"

"What do you mean, *my little microphone*?"

"Look at you in that one," said Franny. "Flipping the switch for the millions of twinkle lights at Winter Wonderland."

"I believe that was . . ." Owen grabbed the stack of photos and flipped through it. "Yes, here it is. That was right before you led the first round of skating at the faux ice skating rink."

"But . . ." Alice started to say.

"No buts about it," said Owen. "You *like* to be in charge. Admit it."

Alice reclaimed the photos, flipped through them, and

found the one of the three friends at the end of the 5k. "I guess being in charge is kind of like running a race. It feels awful while you're doing it, but you get a strange sense of accomplishment when it's over."

Owen and Franny thought about this for a moment and nodded.

"We accept that answer," said Owen, stoking up the fire in the small fire ring they had added to the garden the year before. "Now. Let's talk about New Year's Eve," he said.

"It's going to be the best one ever," said Franny, grabbing her leather backpack and pulling out a crisp, white invitation with dark green lettering. "Because we'll all be together at the lodge."

The lodge—a.k.a. the Great Granddaddy Mountain Preserve and Resort Lodge—was a brand new addition to the town. Phase One had just been completed, and the entire town, along with a few out-of-town visitors, was invited to the grand opening party on New Year's Eve. Even Alice, who wasn't one for big parties, was excited about the event.

"I can't wait to see the nature trails," she said. "I've heard there's going to be a bonfire in the woods."

"And stargazing," said Franny with a sigh.

"And cake," added Owen, who had been contracted by the lodge to create a spectacular cake, which would include five tiers arranged on different levels, featuring the winter constellations in shimmering gold icing, set against a midnight blue fondant background. On one of the tiers, the words "Happy New Year" would be spelled out in metallic copper-colored stars. The whole creation would be wrapped in a string of tiny gold lights to set off the sparkling icing. "I'm bringing my new camera," said Owen. "That way I can get plenty of shots of the finished cake for the bakery blog and website."

"We should definitely get a shot of the senator eating a piece!" said Alice.

"Ooh, you're right," said Owen. "I can see it on the front page of the *Post* now: 'Senator Says, Let Them Eat Cake.'"

State Senator Adam Matthews was the celebrity guest who'd been booked for the lodge's grand opening, and he was the perfect match for the event. Both he and his wife, Nan, were outspoken supporters of environmental preservation, and the lodge had been built around that theme.

"I hear the Fenders are good friends of the senator and his wife," said Franny.

Chad Fender, the developer of the lodge, was a thirty-something, nature-loving, granola-toting hipster, and Alice, Owen, and Franny had gotten to be friends with him since he'd followed his dream and moved to Blue Valley to stay. Chad's wife—whom nobody had laid eyes on as yet—was a rising-star architect. Together, they'd created a master plan that was both luxurious and comfortable, that protected and honored the environment, but also served as an upscale getaway for discerning travelers. There had been a lot of mystery surrounding the lodge because almost no one had yet been allowed to see it other than those who were helping to construct it—although Jane Elkin, editor, owner, and reporter for the *Post*, had been covering the development with weekly articles.

"Anybody home?"

Alice's heart beat faster at the sound of Luke Evans' voice. He and her brother emerged from Alice's apartment and came out into the garden.

"Honey, I'm home," Ben said to Franny, giving her a peck on the cheek. "Alice, your door was unlocked," he added, giving Alice his sternest big-brother look.

Alice never locked the front door of her apartment when Ben and Luke were coming over—although, she always locked the bookstore downstairs, and had given both Ben and Luke keys to that door. At the back of the first floor was a hallway which was accessible from each of the three shops, and in the hallway was a beautiful old wooden staircase that led to a landing above, and the three apartment doors.

Alice's cat, Poppy, immediately ran out into the garden and jumped into Ben's lap as he took his seat next to his wife.

"For crying out loud, Poppy!" said Ben, as the cat rubbed a whiskered cheek against his chin, purring loudly.

"How was work today?" Franny asked.

"Another crime-free day," said Ben.

"Yep, you can all rest easy tonight," said Luke. "The town is secure."

"What about the rash of crime in the park I read about?" asked Alice.

"You mean the popcorn bandit? We solved that," said Ben.

"Really? So, who was taking people's popcorn?" asked Franny.

"A small gang of chipmunks," said Ben.

"How adorable is that? I can just see them now, being taken down to the station in tiny handcuffs," said Owen.

"We found we could pretty much leave the chipmunks alone if people would just stop leaving popcorn lying around," said Luke. "Ever since Ollie Watson started parking his Kernel Pop's Popcorn cart in the park, it's been mayhem."

Luke was Blue Valley PD's detective. He'd moved to the town from Nashville about a year and a half ago, and had literally swept Alice off her feet—or knocked her down, more accurately—shortly after his arrival. Alice's first impression of Luke was not the best—although she'd certainly appreciated his rugged good looks right from the get-go. Where Ben was a kind of studious, sweet handsome, and Owen was a kind of polished, charming handsome, Luke was an outdoorsy, intense kind of handsome. When she'd first met him, Alice would never have dreamed that a year and a half later, she'd be very much in love with him.

"We were just talking about the party at the lodge," said Franny, pouring mugs of hot cocoa for Ben and Luke.

"Tomorrow night," said Ben, nodding. "New Year's Eve already."

"Alice and I are going over there early to help Owen deliver and assemble the cake," said Franny. "We need to get there around four o'clock. You two can meet us there at five."

"It'll be good to see Chad," said Ben.

"And finally meet his wife," added Franny.

"Roz Fender," mused Owen. When all heads turned his way, he added, "I've never met the woman in person. She was the one who arranged for the cake, so I talked to her on the phone. And via email. And text messages. She even faxed me once."

"Really? All over one cake?" asked Alice.

"The woman is some kind of famous architect," said Owen. "She's a creative, like me. Very . . . what's the word?"

"Micromanage-y?" asked Alice.

"*Particular*," said Owen. "She strikes me as the kind of person who wants things the way she wants them."

"Chad is the poster child for 'laid-back,'" said Alice. "Sounds like his wife is the polar opposite. But then again, opposites do sometimes attract. Maybe she's the yin to his yang."

"That would be the *yang to his yin* in this case," said Owen. "Roz is definitely the yang."

"I'd better be heading home," said Luke, drinking down the last of his cocoa and standing.

Luke lived in a cabin out on the lake, just down Lake Trail from Ben and Franny—when they were in residence there. Alice found herself spending more and more time in Luke's cozy cabin, and even when she wasn't there, she sometimes daydreamed about sitting by the stone fireplace with him, or having dinner on the big back porch, or snuggling into a blanket together down on the dock that overlooked the water.

"We're staying in our town house tonight," said Ben, smiling at Franny.

The lake was a ten-minute bike ride from Main Street, but Franny and Ben sometimes jokingly referred to their tiny apartment over Joe's as their "town house." The police station was half a block away, just up Main and a quick right on Phlox Street. All the streets in Blue Valley were named for wildflowers that grow in the Smokies, so the town map included names like Trout Lilly, Trillium, and Azalea, among many others.

"I'll walk you out," said Alice, following Luke into her apartment, to her door.

He turned back and made a stern face. "Now, you lock this door, Alice Maguire," he said in his all-business voice.

"I will," said Alice, rolling her eyes. "I'll do it right—"

Luke didn't wait for Alice to finish her sentence before grabbing her arm, pulling her close, and kissing her, all in one swift movement.

"Wow," said Alice, after he'd release her.

"That's what I think every time I'm near you," Luke whispered, tucking a curl behind Alice's ear. "*Wow*."

"I'll see you tomorrow at the lodge?"

"Yep."

"Everyone will be there, you know."

"Yep." Luke grinned. "I hope I get a moment alone with you."

"That sounds awfully nice," said Alice.

"I have something I want to ask you."

Alice felt the heat rise into her cheeks. Even though they'd been dating for over a year, Luke still had that effect on her. "What is it?"

"No. Not now," said Luke, stepping through the door and starting down the stairs, a twinkle in his eyes. "Tomorrow night."

CHAPTER 2

"Is Beth covering the coffee shop for the rest of the day?" Alice asked Franny as the two of them stood in the garden the following afternoon, looking down over Main Street.

"Yes, and since we're closed for New Year's Day, I feel like I'm on vacation already."

"You haven't really taken time off since you and Ben's honeymoon in the fall, have you?"

"Nope. Other than Christmas." Franny turned a smile on her friend. "How long has it been since you took a vacation? I mean a real vacation where you aren't in charge of anything."

Alice thought for a moment. "It's been a while," she admitted. "Good thing I love my job." Alice sighed contentedly. "I love my little bookshop. I love it that I get to be around books and book lovers every day. And that I don't have meetings or a lot of stress. And, of course, best of all, I get to work right next door to my two dearest friends in the world."

"And, you have a *very* short commute from home," said Franny with a laugh.

"That's the truth," said Alice. "Now, we'd better get ready to go out to the lodge. What are you wearing?"

"My new sweater and those comfy black leggings I just got. This is the first invitation I've ever gotten that calls for *outdoor casual*."

"Isn't it great?" said Alice. "Can you imagine us in cocktail gowns, taking a nature hike, and standing around a bonfire? That would *not* work."

"Where's Owen, anyway? I know he's excited to break in his new designer hiking boots."

As if on cue, Alice and Franny's cell phones dinged at exactly the same time.

"Speak of the devil," said Alice, reading the text. "He

says he got a call from Roz Fender, and she's on her way to the bakery."

"Now?" asked Franny, shocked. "We're supposed to deliver the cakes out to the lodge in less than an hour. Wonder what she could want."

"We'll soon find out," said Alice, pointing down to Main Street, where a shiny red sports car was just pulling up in front of Sourdough.

"She didn't even park between the lines!" said Franny. "She's taking up two spaces. How rude!"

They watched as a glamorous-looking woman, wearing snug, strategically distressed jeans, a trendy cable-knit, white turtleneck sweater, and knee-high boots with spiky heels, hopped out and hurried into the bakery below. She was followed by a young woman with dark hair pulled back into a messy ponytail, wearing a much more subdued outfit—consisting of a white t-shirt, khaki pants, and a denim jacket. She carried a small notebook and practically had to run to catch up to the first woman.

A few minutes later, Owen emerged onto the sidewalk with the two women, furiously scribbling notes down on his clipboard as the glamorous woman talked.

Then, the two women quickly got back into the sports car and sped away.

As if he could feel his friends watching, Owen looked up to the rooftop garden and gave Alice and Franny an imploring wave to come down.

"What's going on? Was that the enigmatic Roz Fender?" asked Alice as she and Franny joined Owen in the kitchen section of his bakery after giving Hilda, Owen's assistant who was working the front counter, a quick hello.

"Canis Major. That's the problem!" said a flustered Owen.

It was rare to see Owen in such a state. He could be a bit on the dramatic side, to be sure, but not in the bakery. When he was at work in Sourdough, he was calm and focused and creative. Alice was constantly amazed at what Owen could do with a little butter and sugar and flour.

"Canis *what-is*?" asked Franny.

"The great dog," said Alice, nodding. "It's a constellation."

"That's right," said Owen, moving hurriedly around

the large island where each tier of the cake for the party was set out. He finally stopped at one of the tiers. "There it is."

Alice and Franny joined him and looked at the small, shimmering stars that formed the constellation.

"So, what's the problem?" asked Franny.

"Roz wants Canis Major removed to make room for Hercules," said Owen.

"Hercules?" asked Alice, confused. "But, isn't that a summer constellation?"

"Thus, it is not on this cake!" Owen's voice was rising higher with each word.

"You're sounding a little shrill there, Owen," said Alice. "Tell us how we can help."

Owen took a deep breath in an attempt to calm his nerves. "I'm going to scrape these stars off, repair the background, then apply the new stars. Franny, look up Hercules on your phone so I'll know how to place the stars. And Alice, Roz has also decided that she wants the words "Happy New Year" in metallic copper instead of gold." He handed Alice a small bottle of edible food paint and a paint brush. "You have great handwriting, so I know you can do this. Go over the stars that form each letter with the new coloring. Once we've unloaded and assembled the cakes out at the lodge, I'll do the final airbrushing to create the Milky Way. "

Between the three of them, the work went fairly quickly, and then they rushed upstairs to clean up for the party. Half an hour later, they all met out in the garden.

"Everyone ready?" asked Alice, who was last to emerge from her apartment.

"Alice, you look gorgeous!" said Franny.

Alice looked down at her clothes. "I wear this all the time."

"It's not the clothes," said Owen, walking in a little circle around Alice and sizing her up. "You're glowing," he pronounced.

Alice had pulled her auburn curls back into a low, loose ponytail. She was wearing her favorite hazelnut-colored cargo pants with hiking boots and a thick, olive green wool sweater that set off her fair, freckled skin and the green of her eyes. To this, she had added her coziest parka, replete with faux fur-lined hood.

"Why are you glowing, Alice?" Franny teased, a big smile on her face.

"I wonder if it has anything to do with a certain Detective Hot Stuff," Owen ventured.

Alice could tell her face had turned the color of a ripe red apple. "Luke said he wanted to ask me something tonight," she said, trying to sound casual.

"Wonder what that could be," Owen said with a knowing grin.

"You can wonder on the way to the lodge," said Alice. "We've got to get those cakes loaded up."

"Before Roz changes her mind again!" said Owen with a roll of his eyes.

"Should I grab my heavy coat, do you think?" Franny asked, eyeing Alice's parka.

"We'll be outside a good bit tonight," said Alice. "And, it feels like snow."

"*Feels* like snow?" Owen looked at the mostly blue sky and then checked the weather app on his phone.

"Nope. Not tonight," he said, scrolling through the forecast. "There's a big storm to the north, but it's going to miss us entirely."

"I don't know . . ." said Alice, eyeing the clouds gathering far off to the north. "I've lived here for over thirty years now, and—"

"Alice, you were *born* here," said Owen. "It's not as though you were observing the weather as a toddler."

"What are you saying? I can't take credit for the whole thirty years?"

"Just saying," said Owen, walking back toward his apartment.

"It definitely *smells* like snow," said Franny, sniffing the air.

"There! You see? Franny's nose is never wrong!" said Alice triumphantly.

"She's probably smelling the melting snow that's already on the ground. Or, the snow that's over there, to the north," said Owen, waving a hand in a general northerly direction.

"I just—I have a feeling about tonight," said Alice.

"What? You're clairvoyant now? You're the cloud whisperer?" said Owen with a laugh.

"We'd better be on our way, you two," said Franny. "I have a feeling Roz Fender doesn't take kindly to tardiness."

"Good point. Let's go," said Owen, and he and Franny hurried into his apartment to head downstairs to the bakery.

But Alice stopped and took a last look at the distant clouds. She shook her head and pulled her coat a little bit tighter around herself.

"There's definitely a storm coming," she muttered, and followed her friends inside.

CHAPTER 3

It was exactly four o'clock when Alice, Owen, and Franny entered the grounds of the Great Granddaddy Mountain Preserve and Resort Lodge.

"Wow. This is just the driveway," said Franny, as they all marveled at the road that wove through the woods and deeper into the valley. There was a collective gasp from the three of them as the trees cleared and they saw the lodge for the first time. It was set in a beautiful clearing, in the shadow of Great Granddaddy Mountain. The main building lay straight ahead, and looked, somehow, as if it had been there for a hundred years.

"Part log cabin, part mountain lodge, part something

else," said Owen, looking up at the gorgeous structure.

"New England!" said Alice. "That's the something else! Look—there's a widow's walk on top."

"Look at that huge balcony on the second floor!" said Franny. "And the front entry!"

Owen pulled his SUV into the parking lot near the service entrance, as Roz had instructed him to do, and the three carefully unloaded cake boxes and took them into the kitchen.

"Who might you be?" A man with a thick French accent looked up from a large workstation in the middle of the kitchen. Around him, a half dozen men and women worked quietly, chopping things, sautéing things, sliding things into the oven. Alice's stomach growled audibly at the delicious smells.

"You must be Chef Boucher," said Owen, hurrying over to shake the man's hand.

"I am, yes," the man answered. "Louis Boucher."

"Owen James," said Owen. "I've read about your work. Nice to meet you."

"Of course. Mr. James," said the chef, his small waxed mustache curling up with his smile. "I take it these are your lovely helpers." He looked at Alice and Franny and sent them a charming grin.

"Yes," said Owen. "This is Alice and Franny Maguire."

"Sisters, is it?"

"No," said Owen. "Franny recently married Alice's brother."

"Sisters, then," said Chef Louis, a twinkle in his eye. "You may set up the cakes in the ballroom. The first door, there, is the kitchen entrance. You will see the cake table off to one side."

"Thank you, chef," said Owen.

"But of course," said Chef Louis. "You may leave your coats in the coat closet if you wish. It is near the large entryway, just off the great room—where the guests check in. The signs will point the way."

It only took a few trips from the car, through the kitchen, into the ballroom for the three friends to get all of the cake tiers safely to the cake table. The layout of the first floor, from the standpoint of usability, was impeccable. The kitchen was a long, wide corridor of a room that ran along one end. It had banks of windows along one wall, bringing in lots of natural light where chefs and sous chefs worked at long counters, chopping and washing and arranging. From the kitchen, there were entries directly into the ballroom, the dining room, and a corridor that led to the great room.

The ballroom, which would be well-suited to wedding receptions, parties, and large meetings or conventions, was nothing like the usual bland hotel facilities Alice had seen before. It had gleaming natural wood floors and there was a stone fireplace angled into a corner. The room was mostly cleared of furniture, since there would be a dance that night, and there was a small, raised platform in one corner where the band would presumably set up. The ceiling was strung with drapes of old-fashioned lightbulbs that cast a warm, cozy glow over the whole room.

"I can take our coats and put them in the coat closet," said Alice, as Owen began the painstaking task of tiering the cakes. He'd brought a small kit with extra tools and icings pre-dyed in the colors of the cake so that he could make any repairs necessary after everything was arranged.

"Thanks," said Owen, as he and Franny peeled out of their coats and scarves and piled them into Alice's arms.

"Want me to check your purse, too, Franny?" Alice asked, nodding at Franny's brown leather backpack.

"No, thanks," Franny said. "Never know when I might need it."

"What do you keep in that thing, anyway?" asked Owen, as Franny dug down into the bag and produced a roll of mints. "It's *huge*."

"I keep *everything* in here," Franny answered. "Mint?"

Owen accepted a mint and turned back to his work.

With a laugh, Alice trotted off, exiting the ballroom and entering the great room for the first time. It was breathtaking, and one of the most thoughtfully designed spaces she'd ever seen, from its exposed beams to its massive stone fireplace—a huge version of the smaller one she'd seen in the ballroom. To the left of the fireplace was a towering Christmas tree, decorated simply in glimmering lights. On closer inspection, Alice could see that the tree was potted, and a small sign on a stand next to it explained that the Fraser fir would be planted on the grounds following the holiday season.

Various cozy seating areas were tucked about the room . . . places to sit by the fire, quiet alcoves to read a good book, larger seating areas for gathering and playing games. In the corner, an upright piano invited impromptu singalongs. Somehow, it all blended together to bring warmth and intimacy to what was actually a very large space. The wall opposite the ballroom doors, facing Great Granddaddy Mountain, was nothing but windows, from the rustic wooden floor to the high ceiling. The panorama was breathtaking—literally.

Alice gave herself a little shake and tore her eyes away from the mesmerizing view and looked around. To the right of the fireplace, there was a grand staircase, with wide, polished wood steps leading up to a railed landing that overlooked the great room. The railing was wrapped in evergreen garland intertwined with twinkling white lights—and the doors to the lodge rooms where guests would stay lined the back wall, each one hung with a different wreath. The staircase then doubled back on itself, heading up to the third level and, presumably, it then continued on up to the widow's walk that Alice had spotted earlier. Alice found herself wishing they could all stay overnight as she looked up the stairway.

She brought her attention back down to where she stood in the great room. Up ahead was the front entryway, with its thick windowed doors and spectacular blown-glass light fixture hanging overhead. Opposite the great room was the guest check-in area, which, like everything else, looked both beautiful and functional. There was an open door that led into an office area behind the check-in counter, and tucked down at the end of the counter, a door labeled "coat check."

Alice hurried through the door and flipped on the light to find a generous space with rows of racks and numbered cubbies for accessories that people might want to set aside, like gloves and purses and hats. Alice had just begun hanging the coats when she heard voices coming from the check-in area. She peeked out of the closet, hoping it was the Fenders, so that she could say hello.

Sure enough, she saw Chad, but his back was to her and then he walked into the office behind the counter, where the person he was speaking to apparently was.

Alice decided to wait until later to speak to the Fenders and went back into the coat closet.

She was shocked when the voices became more audible—*a lot* more audible, as Chad and a woman had now begun to yell at one another.

"You heard me, Chad! We're through! It's over."

"But Roz, I don't understand! Why?"

"If you really insist on knowing—not that it matters anymore—it's because we were never suited for one another! You know that, right?" Her tone had turned ugly. Derogatory. Alice could almost hear the sneer in Roz's voice. "I'm serving you with the papers on Monday. I didn't want you to be surprised."

"Didn't want—" Chad pounded something. The wall, Alice guessed. "Why are you telling me this *now*, Roz? *Right* before the guests start arriving? At the grand opening? What kind of person are you?"

"I'm the kind of person who doesn't want to live next to a mountain in a town that has, what? Three traffic lights?"

There was a long pause, then Chad said, "Fine. You want to leave? Leave. Leave now."

"You'd like that, wouldn't you? You could take all the credit for my design! *My* masterpiece! Sorry, Chad. I'm leaving Monday. This place is half mine, remember—and maybe even more than half mine, because I created it!"

"You? *You* created it? It was my idea! My concept! You can't leave! You know I'll be ruined if you take half of everything before it's even off the ground! Completely ruined!"

"I don't care if you're ruined, actually." Roz's voice was hateful now.

"Roz, when did you decide all of this? What happened? I still don't understand. Please. We can try counseling. We can—"

"*We* aren't going to do anything, Chad. *I* am going up to change before the guests arrive. *I* am going to get out of this God-forsaken town and go back to LA where I belong!"

"But Roz—"

"Get out of my way!"

"But—"

"*Move!*"

Alice felt sick as she heard the rapidly retreating footsteps of Roz, followed by the slow, weary footsteps of Chad. She peeked out of the closet, feeling a mix of horror and guilt that she'd witnessed the exchange. Chad was standing, looking in the direction Roz had gone, mumbling to himself.

Alice felt panicked, not wanting to stay trapped in the closet, but also not wanting to walk out and let Chad know she'd heard his argument with his wife. She was just about to step out with the plan of smiling and pretending she hadn't heard a thing, when Chad's fist came down hard on the counter.

To Alice's relief, he stalked away—but just before he moved out of earshot, she heard him say, "I wish you were dead."

CHAPTER 4

Alice crept out of the coat closet and peered into the entryway. She breathed a sigh of relief on seeing that the coast was clear. Chad was on the far side of the great room, walking up the stairs.

"Whoa. This place is amazing!"

Alice turned to see Ben, followed by Luke, walking in through the front doors.

"Hi, Ben." She looked past her brother and locked eyes with Luke, who looked more handsome than ever in khakis, boots, and a plaid button-up in earthy colors layered under a worn, brown leather jacket. He looked like a walking ad for Eddie Bauer or LL Bean.

"Come on. Let's . . ." Ben looked back and forth between Alice and Luke for a moment. "Oh! I see Franny over there!" He quickly made himself scarce and joined Owen and Franny, who had just emerged from the ballroom.

"Hello, beautiful," Luke said, stepping close to Alice.

It was as if, at that moment, all the clouds cleared from the sky, and golden, late-afternoon light poured through the entryway windows. Alice felt as though she and Luke were the only two people in the entire world, and he seemed to sense it, too, because there was a look of wonder in his eyes.

"Alice, I—I've been wanting to ask you this for a while now, but I wanted the perfect moment." Luke looked around them, then back at Alice. He touched her cheek and looked so deeply into her eyes that Alice almost looked away.

But she didn't.

"This seems like a really perfect moment," she whispered. Then swallowed. She could almost hear the question she hoped Luke would ask—could almost hear herself answering him—when another sound interrupted her thoughts.

"Oh my gosh! It's just beautiful!"

It was Bea Maguire. Just behind her was Martin. And just behind him was Granny and Chester Lehman. Alice's whole family had basically filled the entryway, and she could see another small group ambling up the stone path just outside the doors behind them. There was Pearl Ann Dowry, who owned the Blue Beauty Spa, and her longtime beau, Norman McKenzie who owned and operated Odd Job Bob, a handyman service. Behind them, Alice could see Doug and Barb Blake, who owned the gourmet chocolate shop, Sugarbuzz, and George and Izzie Whitman, of Whitman's Grocery.

As her family moved off into the great room, oohing and aahing all the way, Alice knew she had only seconds alone with Luke before the next group entered the lodge. "You were saying?" she asked, trying to recapture his full attention and the magical moment.

Luke grinned and gave Alice a peck on the cheek. "Later," he whispered. "We should go say hello."

"Gather 'round, everyone!" Roz Fender was standing

next to the fireplace, motioning for the growing group of guests to join her.

Everyone gathered into the space, and Alice noticed half the town had showed up, everyone in the same state of awe at the beauty of the lodge and the view of the Smoky Mountains outside.

"On behalf of myself and my husband, Chad, hello, and welcome to the Great Granddaddy Mountain Preserve and Resort Lodge!" She gave a little snicker. "Whew! That was a mouthful! My husband named the lodge, and he is a man of many words." She directed everyone's attention to Chad, who had just come back down the stairs and gave a smile and a wave before joining the group. "We thought we'd start with a little meet-and-greet," Roz continued. "You've already met Chad, of course. I am Roz, the architect who designed this beautiful place—pardon me for bragging. We'd also like you to meet Michael Boyd, our concierge."

From the crowd, an impeccably dressed man with smiling eyes and rich brown skin stepped forward. "It will be my pleasure to assist you with anything you need during your stay here," he said, giving a wave.

"Later, you'll all be sampling the delectable work of our amazing chef, the award-winning Louis Boucher!" Roz continued.

Chef Louis waved at the crowd. "I would also like to thank my excellent staff and your own Mr. Owen James, who has provided the exquisite cake you will enjoy later tonight."

Alice and Franny looked at Owen, who was fairly beaming at the compliment.

"And now, we'd like you to meet our very special guests for the evening: Senator Adam Matthews, and his lovely wife, Nan." Roz waved to a handsome couple standing just to the other side of the fireplace.

"Just look at them!" Owen, who was standing next to Alice, whispered. "They're gorgeous!"

"Look at their clothes!" Franny whispered, from Alice's other side. "So glamorous!"

"I know," said Alice. "I mean, they're dressed casually, but somehow they look so chic. How did they do that?"

"Gertrude Alderman, that's how," said Owen.

"Who?" asked Alice.

"Gertrude Alderman. The fashion designer? Duh!"

"Never heard of her," said Alice. "So that's what they're wearing?"

"Her sweater. Her shoes. His pants. His jacket." Owen sighed. "I've had that jacket on my fashion wish list since last fall, when it was launched."

"It's a nice tweed jacket," said Alice.

This comment got her a look of dismay from Owen. "That's not just tweed, my dear Alice. That's a hopsack weave in the finest Irish wool. Notice the color variation within the weave. It also has four internal pockets and a double-vented back. Every jacket is bespoke. One of a kind." Owen let out a small whimper of envy.

"Maybe my parents will get you that jacket on your birthday." Alice teased.

As Alice, Owen, and Franny catalogued the couple's clothing, the senator was just wrapping up a short welcome message of his own, where he mentioned the Fenders' care for the environment as they'd built the lodge.

"What did he say?" Owen whispered.

"No idea," said Alice. "We were too busy looking at their clothes."

"Speaking of: Get a load of Roz's necklace," said Franny. "It's so beautiful! What's that symbol?"

Alice squinted at the necklace, which shimmered brilliantly every time the sunlight from the great windows caught on it. It looked to be made entirely of tiny diamonds, and was composed of three curved branches, curling out from its center. "Oh. That's called a triskele," she said. "It's an ancient Celtic symbol."

"What does it mean?" asked Franny.

"It means different things to different people," said Alice. "It can symbolize the interconnectedness of the realms of earth, water, and sky, for instance."

"I love it when she talks history," said Luke, putting an arm around Alice as they were herded from the great room to the staircase.

From the second-floor landing, Roz took one group of guests, Chad took another, and Roz's assistant, Sadie Green, took the third, with each group going off in its own direction. Alice and her family were in Sadie's group.

"She's so adorable with her little notebook," said Owen.

"Sharp as a tack, too," said Alice, as Sadie answered someone's question about load-bearing beams.

The lodge got more impressive with every turn, every level. The view from the huge second-floor balcony was amazing, but when the group emerged onto the modern-day widow's walk on the top of the building, a hush fell over the chatty bunch.

Great Granddaddy Mountain—and all of the surrounding mountains—stood proud and green and snow-spangled against a brilliant blue sky. A bracing wind felt like a chilly rush of refreshment in Alice's face as she looked around in amazement. She had never felt more grateful to live in this beautiful valley.

As the group descended back down to the first floor, Alice, Owen, and Franny caught up with Sadie.

"This place is just amazing," Alice told her.

Sadie smiled shyly. "We think so, too," she said, her dark, almond eyes crinkling with delight.

"So, you're Roz's assistant?" Franny asked.

"Yes. I've been with her for five years now, since I finished grad school."

"Oh—what did you study?" asked Alice.

"Architecture," said Sadie. "I'm interning with Roz, learning everything I can."

"That's wonderful," said Franny.

Sadie gave them another smile and directed everyone back into the great room, where the other two tour groups had already arrived.

The senator stepped forward again. "Before we all go in to dinner, I have the great honor of making a special announcement," he said, his voice clear and deep above the chatter of the crowd. Everyone stopped talking and listened. "I have just been told that Roz Fender has been nominated for the prestigious Ellison Field Award for Excellence in Environmentally Sustainable Architecture for the design of this amazing place!"

The crowd broke into applause, and if Alice hadn't been standing right next to Sadie, she wouldn't have heard her release a small gasp.

"What an honor," Alice said, looking at Sadie.

"What? Oh, yes! A huge honor!" said Sadie, holding her notebook to her chest.

"And now, let's all go in and enjoy Chef Louis' dinner!" said Roz.

They were shown into a huge dining room that lay directly on the other side of the great room—which allowed the two rooms to share the massive fireplace.

A gorgeous long, polished oak table was set with china and crystal and too many candles to count. From the ceiling hung what looked like thousands of crystal snowflakes, each one glistening in the fire and candlelight. There was a place card for each guest. Alice, Franny, and Owen were seated next to each other, and Alice was happy that Luke was seated directly across the table from her. Ben sat across from Franny. Owen was delighted to have Granny Maguire across from him.

On the menu that night were five courses: the amuse bouche course consisted of seared scallops and tiny roasted root vegetables. That was followed by a crisp salad, a creamy pasta with black truffles and crispy garlic, a pan seared fresh-caught trout almondine, and finally, a selection of fine cheeses and fruits. Chef Louis was summoned for a bow at the end of the meal, and he received a boisterous round of applause.

"Here's to the best chef this side of the Smokies," said Roz, raising a glass of wine.

After glasses were clinked and sips of wine were taken, Owen leaned over to Alice and Franny. "Anyone else notice that old Roz has been hitting the wine a bit hard this evening?"

"She does sound a little tipsy," said Franny. "And it's only seven thirty."

"I bet I know why," whispered Alice. "She and Chad had a big fight earlier."

"And you know this because . . ." Owen said, raising a brow at Alice.

"I overheard the whole thing. From the coat closet," said Alice. "She said she was going to leave Chad. That she's serving the papers on Monday. Isn't that sad?" Alice looked at Chad, who was seated next to his wife, and to all outward appearances, seemed fine. "I'm surprised Chad's not the one drinking too much wine."

"Why?" asked Owen.

"Because he said he'll be ruined if she leaves him." Alice lowered her whisper even further. "And, he said he wished she was dead."

This met with looks of shock from Owen and Franny, along with "Seriously?" and "Harsh!"

"They do seem ill-suited, though," admitted Franny.

"I wonder how they met," said Alice.

"I can answer that," said Owen. "Because my end of the table has been discussing it."

"Spill," said Franny.

"We don't know the whole story," said Owen, glancing briefly over his shoulder at the group of locals nearest him, which included Pearl Ann, who knew everything about everybody, their uncle, *and* their uncle's uncle. "But we do know that Chad was supposed to be Roz's transitional man."

"Her transitional man? As in, she rebounded into him?" asked Franny.

"Everyone knows you're not supposed to *marry* your transitional man," said Owen sagely. "*Big* no-no."

"I wonder who Roz was with before she married Chad," said Franny.

"You two are horrible. Who cares?" said Alice.

"Well, that brings us to the juicy part," said Owen, leaning over Alice and giving Franny a conspiratorial grin. "The other odd couple here tonight—the couple who doesn't seem like a logical pairing—is the senator and his wife."

Alice rolled her eyes as Owen and Franny subtly looked to the end of the table where the Matthews were seated.

"Go on," said Franny, biting into a small wedge of cheese.

"Adam Matthews, the senator, dated Roz Fender before he married Nan!"

"He was who Roz was rebounding from!" said Franny.

"Oh, for crying out loud!" said Alice, begrudgingly entering the conversation. "Look at Nan! She clearly adores her husband."

"Just saying," said Owen, holding up his hands innocently. "Pearl Ann says Adam and Roz were quite an item, but then they broke up, and each married a different person fairly soon thereafter."

"And now the four of them are seated at opposite ends of this table," said Alice.

"Aaawk-waard," sang Owen.

"Apparently, things aren't going so well between Chad and Roz," said Franny. "So, maybe it's all true, and you really shouldn't marry your transitional man."

Alice glanced down the table at Adam and Nan, then casually turned the other direction to look at Roz and Chad. She noticed that Roz kept looking down in Adam's direction. Alice shook her head. "Trouble in paradise."

CHAPTER 5

"Ha! I told you it would snow!" Alice said as they all stepped out into the wintery evening.

"You call this snow?" Owen scoffed. "Nah! These are just teaser flakes. They won't even stick. You'll see."

"Want to make a bet?"

"Alice. Meteorology is an exact science. To take that bet would be unfair to you." He glanced over at Franny. "And even to Franny's mystical sense of smell."

A chilly breeze swept across the entryway.

"I'm going back for my parka," said Alice.

"Me, too," said Franny.

The breeze swirled around them, blowing a little funnel of leaves across the lawn.

"I guess it couldn't hurt," said Owen.

They left the group—most of whom had bundled up before exiting the lodge—and hurried into the check-in area and coat closet. When they emerged, they saw Sadie and Roz, standing behind the front desk, and Roz was clearly not happy.

"I told you a million times, Sadie! I wanted the extra-large marshmallows. Not the regular-sized ones! How could you be so stupid?"

"I'm sorry. There were none at the store. Those were the largest they had."

"Then you should've special ordered them!"

"You didn't specify until two days before the opening. There wouldn't have been time to—"

"I don't want to hear it! Not one more word!"

Sadie opened her mouth, then closed it in defeat. This seemed to appease Roz, who walked off in a huff and went outside to join the group where, even from inside, she could be heard welcoming everyone to the candlelit hike in her happiest voice.

"What a witch!" Owen said, approaching Sadie, who still stood silently in the same spot. But now, her cheeks glistened with tears. "How can you stand to work for that woman?"

Sadie hastily wiped her cheeks and turned bright red, seeing that three people had just witnessed her chastisement. "I really messed up," she said. "Sorry you had to hear that."

"Messed up by getting the wrong marshmallows?" Alice shook her head. "That's not a big deal, Sadie. No one should be talked to like that."

Owen put a comforting hand on Sadie's back and handed her the box of tissues from the desk. "She was awful to me, too."

"Owen! You didn't say!" Alice said.

"Yep," Owen continued. "I mean, I didn't want to make a big thing of it. But about the cakes: It wasn't just that Roz was picky. She was mean. I wanted the gig, so I put up with it. I can't even imagine having to deal with her all the time." He looked back at Sadie.

"I need the reference. For all of her faults, Roz is a famous architect."

"You said you've been her intern for five years! Isn't that a bit long? Where did you go to school?" asked Alice.

"M.I.T.," said Sadie, blowing her nose. "Part of my master's degree was an internship. Then, I become a licensed architect and can finally break away from Roz. But she keeps dragging the whole process out. I've invested so much time with her . . . I can't leave now. You have to pay your dues in this line of work."

"What a price to pay!" said Owen.

Sadie nodded. "But, I'm grateful for the experience."

They all moved together outside, where the group was walking toward a candlelit trail up ahead.

"The experience of doing what? Buying marshmallows?" Owen whispered, craning his neck to locate Roz, who was up at the front of the group, along with Chad, the senator, and Nan.

"Does Roz let you do actual architecture work? Did you help with the design of the lodge?" asked Alice.

At this question, a small furrow appeared between Sadie's brows, then vanished. "Oh, no," she said nervously, her eyes moving ahead to the front of the group. "I am currently designing a lovely, um, garden shed, though." She patted the little notebook she carried. "Roz has talked about letting me work on a convenience store floor plan, so . . . I'm hoping that works out."

"Is that where you keep your designs?" Franny asked, gesturing toward the notebook.

Sadie looked down at the notebook and nodded. "All of my ideas and inspirations go in here. Sketches. Brainstorms. That's why I keep it with me at all times. You never know when the big ideas will come."

"Can we see some of your sketches?" Owen asked, playfully elbowing Sadie, who finally smiled again.

"Oh, no! No one looks at this. These are just . . . ideas." She smiled at all three of them. "Thank you for cheering me up. I'd better get down the trail. I need to make sure everything's ready in the clearing."

"The clearing?" asked Franny.

"Where we're having the bonfire!" Sadie called back over her shoulder as she veered onto a different trail. "See you up there!"

"Well, that was interesting," said Owen after Sadie had disappeared into the woods.

"Poor girl," said Franny. "I'd like to give that Roz a good, swift kick in the—"

"And now, we will relax and enjoy the hike. Let's go catch up with Ben and Luke," said Alice.

Ben and Luke were deep in conversation with the Maguire parents up near the front of the pack. Alice caught hold of Luke's hand, and he smiled warmly.

"There you are," he said, squeezing her hand.

A small movement out of the corner of Alice's eye caught her attention. She turned, expecting to see a chipmunk or squirrel in the trees, but instead, saw Roz and the senator, walking in the shadows just off the trail. Alice was pretty sure she saw Roz reach for his hand. Alice looked away quickly, then a moment later, subtly turned her head to check again. But the senator was moving on ahead, out of the trees, and then he stepped back out onto the trail.

Alice sought out Nan in the group and saw that she seemed to be enjoying a chat with Pearl Ann and Norman. When her husband approached, she turned a beaming smile on him and took his arm.

A few minutes later, the woods opened up into a clearing, where a bonfire snapped and crackled, creating a warm circle of light. Trays laden with marshmallows, chocolate bars, and a selection of cookies and graham crackers were passed around, along with skewers. The guests were also invited to look through the telescope that had been erected just beyond the fire.

Alice and Luke stepped over to the telescope.

"It's getting cloudy," said Alice, peering through the lens. "But I can still see a few stars up there."

Luke took a deep breath of the cold, fresh air. "This place is amazing," he said, looking all around. "We'll have to come back again sometime."

Alice smiled at him. "I'd love that."

He stepped closer and pulled her into his arms, took a

quick look back at the crowd around the bonfire, and then kissed her.

At that moment, the snow began to fall. Ironically, Alice realized that she no longer felt cold. Not in the least.

"This is the perfect night," Luke said, looking at the fluffy flakes drifting in the air.

Alice closed her eyes and turned her smile toward the moon, which had just peeked through the clouds to illuminate the snowflakes. She felt what could only be called elation. And not because of any promise of the future. Not because of the "Question" Luke had hinted at. Just because the moment itself was pure magic—between the loved ones gathered around, the snow, the air, the mountains. Alice loved her life. Future and past faded away, leaving only this perfect present moment on this snowy night. Just then, an owl who'd been hidden by tree boughs took flight and swooped past them, only a few yards away.

Alice gasped in amazement.

"Owls all over Tennessee probably revere you because you named your bookstore after them," said Luke, kissing her hair. He pulled back a little and looked at her, and Alice had the sense that he was feeling as full and as joyful as she was. He opened his mouth to speak, when suddenly, a bright light flashed in their faces.

"Say cheese!"

"Owen!"

"Hey, you'll thank me when you have a framed four-by-six to commemorate this moment."

"Did you see the great horned owl?" Alice's dad hurried over.

"I certainly did," said Owen.

"Let's try to follow it. See if we can get a few good photos. Is your flash working?"

Owen smiled. "Yep. I just tested it out on Alice and Luke here."

"Let's go," Martin said, and they hurried off in the direction the owl had gone.

"How about a toasted marshmallow?" Luke asked, as he and Alice walked back to the bonfire.

"After a five-course meal, that's about all I have room for," Alice said with a laugh.

Luke took her hand. "Midnight," he said softly, as if talking to himself.

"What?"

Luke grinned and shook his head. "Nothing."

CHAPTER 6

By the time the group made its way back to the lodge around nine o'clock, the snow was coming down in earnest. Big, fat flakes were falling—and sticking to the ground . . . and beginning to form small drifts here and there. Owen cursed his weather app and was forced to admit that Alice's gut and Franny's nose had been right.

"I don't know why you would question my wisdom," said Alice.

"And now, if you will all step into the ballroom, we'll enjoy dessert and crack open the champagne!" Roz announced.

Owen's creation received a well-earned round of

applause. Before the cakes were cut, everyone admired them, pointing out the different constellations and marveling at the swirls of color in the Milky Way. People could be overheard asking Owen about ordering customized party cakes and wondering at how the tiny twinkle lights set off the metallic frosting. The praise didn't stop when the cake was cut and served, and people found that it tasted even more wonderful than it looked. Owen took photo after photo of people happily enjoying their cake, but the senator—although he'd taken a generous slice—eluded Owen's lens. Every time he'd start to take a bite, another person would walk up to him to say hello or shake his hand or ask him a question. Owen's quest for the perfect photo became almost laughable when the senator set down his cake to speak to a guest, and Zeb Clark, the local coroner, also set down his cake to get a cup of coffee. Then, Zeb's wife picked up Zeb's slice, thinking it was hers, and finally, Zeb, looking around for his own slice, walked off with the senator's. Owen quickly rectified the matter by bringing the senator a second slice, but still couldn't catch him eating it.

"Ooh! Get your camera ready, Owen!" Alice said, as the senator finally loaded a forkful of cake.

Owen fumbled with his lens cover and had just focused in when Roz, who seemed to be more interested in the champagne than the cake, called the senator to join her by the ballroom's fireplace.

"I know you'd all love to hear a little bit from Adam —Senator Matthews—about his latest legislative proposal for the preservation of this very land and more like it!"

There was a round of applause, and the senator was obliged to set his cake down and address the group.

"*Why won't he eat the cake?*" Owen groaned from where he, Alice, and Franny stood, toward the back of the group.

"Who knows? Personally, I can't get enough of it!" said Franny, taking a big bite of her third piece.

"People keep interrupting him," whispered Alice. "Every time he tries, someone grabs him. It must be awful to be a politician."

"And now, let's *really* get this party started!" Roz announced, after the senator had finished his impromptu speech.

That must've been the band's signal, because they

began to play the first song. The Fenders and the Matthews took to the dance floor immediately, encouraging others to join them.

"Hold it. Isn't that the Gothic Trolls? The same band that played at the medieval faire last spring?" asked Owen, raising a brow at the band.

Sure enough, Dante Johansen, the Trolls' lead singer, had traded his dulcimer for an electric guitar, and Fenrir Larsen had swapped out his lute for a set of drums. Sía Olsen was still playing the harp—but she was rocking it. The band had an entirely different sound than they had at the medieval faire and was currently playing their own rousing rendition of "Mustang Sally."

"Come on, Owen! Let's show them our new moves!" Granny Maguire said, grabbing Owen by the arm and leading him toward the dance floor.

"New moves?" Alice called after them.

"We've been taking lessons!" Owen called back over his shoulder.

Granny, who lived in a house on Azalea Street just a block off Main, had been traveling the world for the past few years. But, she'd come home over the summer for Ben and Franny's wedding, and surprisingly, had stayed put—for the time being, anyway. That made Alice very happy, because her grandmother was her friend, her hero, and generally, a person who made everything more fun. Granny had come to the party tonight on the arm of her old friend and next-door neighbor, Chester Lehman. But, apparently, during the past few months, she and Owen had been taking dancing lessons—and it showed. They were by far the most exciting couple on the floor.

"Dance with me, Alice?" Luke said, just as Ben grabbed Franny's hand and whisked her away.

Alice felt a little giddy as "Mustang Sally" melded into a slow song, and Luke pulled her close. She rested her chin on his shoulder and marveled at how easily they moved together.

"It's funny. Usually, I have two left feet," she said into his ear. "But dancing with you, I feel like I finally found my right foot."

Luke laughed and kissed Alice's hair.

As they moved about the floor, Alice enjoyed watching the other couples. Norman and Pearl Ann danced like old pros. Alice's parents twirled effortlessly in one another's arms, as they had for forty years now. Doc and Mrs. Howard—the doctor who'd delivered half the people in the room and his wife, who'd taught high school English to at least as many—laughed and talked as they danced.

Then, Alice noticed that Roz Fender had maneuvered herself and Chad over to the corner where the Matthews were dancing and was in the process of swapping partners. The Matthews politely obliged.

Owen and his current partner, Magnolia Anderson, who owned the Parkview Café, quickly danced over to where Alice and Luke were.

"Did you see how Roz cut in just then?" said Owen, a note of gossipy scandal in his voice. "That was bold."

"I know!" Alice answered over Luke's shoulder.

"What are we talking about?" said Franny, who had stepped on Ben's toes a few times as she took the lead to get them over to the same area.

"The way the Fenders and the Matthews just swapped partners," said Owen.

"I know!" said Franny. "If I were that Nan Matthews, I'd give Roz a good swift kick in the shin!"

"Look! Now Chad is asking Sadie to dance!" Owen said.

"You three are horrible!" said Magnolia. "Owen, I'm going for punch."

"So are we," Ben said, taking Luke's arm. "If you three want to whisper together, you should dance together!"

With that, Ben gave Luke a little bow. "Shall we?"

"Why, thank you," said Luke, and the two of them clomped off together in the direction of the punch-bowl in what could be construed as the clumsiest dance anyone had ever witnessed.

Alice, Owen, and Franny, when they'd finally stopped laughing, decided to take some more photos. People who'd been dancing for a while were starting to wander back over to the cake table for seconds.

It was a wonderful evening. The Gothic Trolls turned out to be a huge hit, the party-goers enjoyed dancing, wandering from time to time into the great room to stand by the fire and watch the snow fall from the huge windows, nibbling on cake and sipping champagne. By a quarter past eleven, Alice found herself anticipating the midnight hour with a level of energy she wouldn't have normally felt at that hour.

She and Luke, along with Owen, Franny, and Ben made themselves at home on the cozy couches next to the fire.

"I hope the roads are going to be in decent shape when we head home in a bit," Ben said, looking worriedly at the snow, which was still steadily falling outside.

"If not, we'll just have to stay," said Franny with a laugh.

"But since that is highly unlikely," Owen said. "Everyone stand in front of the fireplace. I want to get a group picture. I'll use my wide-angle lens and capture this gorgeous room."

Just then, Roz, who'd just come out of the ballroom in the company of her husband and Sadie, gave a loud groan. "Chad, I've had too much champagne. I'm going upstairs for a bit."

Alice noticed her shooting a meaningful look in the

direction of Adam, who stood on the other side of the room, quietly talking to his wife. Roz went over to a couple of wingback chairs in a small alcove next to the stairs, picked something up, and then sent one more parting glance at Adam. This time, Alice saw his eyes move over Roz.

"Great! Now, everyone stand over here by the stairs," said Owen.

"Owen! How many pictures do we need to take?" asked Ben.

"Sadie! Could you take a picture of all of us together?" Owen asked.

"Sure," Sadie said, and came over and snapped a few shots.

"You okay?" Alice asked, as Sadie handed the camera back to Owen—who went off gleefully to take more pictures.

"I'm fine. Why?" asked Sadie.

"You look a little gloomy. Just checking," said Alice with a smile.

"I'm fine," Sadie repeated, and looked at the grandfather clock that was set on the wall opposite the fireplace.

"Alice, come here." Owen waved Alice over to the staircase where he and Franny were conspiring. "I've had a fabulous idea. I'm going to film everyone saying their New Year's resolutions! It'll be a hoot!"

"You can shoot videos with that thing, too?"

"Absolutely. Now, come on. It's almost midnight."

Once Owen had filmed Alice and Franny discussing their New Year's hopes and dreams, he went around to all of their friends and family, eliciting the same from them.

"It's eleven forty-five!" said Alice, grabbing Franny's hand and searching through the crowd for Luke. "Almost time to toast the new year! I'll get us some champagne."

"None for me, thanks," said Franny with a yawn. "I think I'll toast with coffee."

"Good idea," said Alice.

"Has anybody seen the Fenders?" Owen asked, scanning the crowd with his telephoto lens. "Surely one of them will want to lead the countdown to midnight in a few minutes."

Alice and Franny looked around. "I don't see either of them," said Alice, frowning, then looking at her watch.

"Somebody has to lead the countdown!" said Franny, as Ben and Luke both emerged from the crowd and joined them.

"I'll ask Senator Matthews!" said Owen, and he hurried off.

Luke took Alice's hand. "Do I really have to wait until midnight to kiss you?" he whispered into her ear.

"Yep," she said, smiling.

Owen returned, panting. "I've looked everywhere. No Fenders. Neither the senator nor his wife is anywhere! What are we going to do? It's literally fifteen minutes to midnight!"

Just then, Sadie wandered by.

"Sadie! Where are the Fenders? We're about to count down!" said Alice.

After looking around the room, Sadie seemed to be as perplexed as everyone else. "Roz will be furious if she misses midnight at her own party. I'll go upstairs and look for them," she said, rushing off.

"Meanwhile, I'll take more pictures!" said Owen, snapping a shot of Alice's parents with Granny and Chester.

A few minutes later, when Sadie still hadn't returned, Alice suggested that they ask Mayor Abercrombie to do the honors. He was very glad to oblige.

"Okay, everyone, let's count down together!" the mayor announced, checking his watch. "Ten! Nine! Eight!"

As the crowd joined in, Alice stepped closer to Luke and looked into his eyes. It almost seemed like they were the only two people in the room.

"Three! Two!"

A blood-curdling scream snapped Alice out of her bubble of romance.

Close on its heels, there was another scream. And then another.

"What's happening?"

Luke immediately switched to detective mode. "Pearl Ann. Was that you screaming?"

"Yes!"

"It was me, too," said Bea, who was standing right beside Ben and Franny, and had turned as white as a sheet.

"What happened?" Ben asked, putting a supportive arm around his mother and easing her to the couch that was right behind them.

"A body," said Bea, a tremor in her voice.

"What? Where?" asked Luke, kneeling down next to Bea.

Bea shakily pointed at the huge windows, where outdoor lights were still illuminating the falling snow. "It fell. Past the windows."

"I saw it, too," said Pearl Ann.

"So did I," said Owen. "I was the third screamer."

"We have to get out there," said Ben.

"Right," said Luke. "Alice, call an ambulance. Ben, I

saw some snow shovels in the front office. Let's grab them and be on our way." He looked through the crowd and spotted the coroner. "Zeb, you'd better come, too. The rest of you folks just stay right here."

But nobody *did* stay right there. Everyone *tried* to stay right there, but in the end, they couldn't see well enough from the windows, and they couldn't subdue their curiosity. After Ben and Luke left, shovels in their hands, the rest of the group gradually donned coats and gloves and trickled casually and quietly out the front door and followed the freshly shoveled path that wound around to the side of the building. Alice was shocked at the depth the snow managed to accumulate while they'd all been inside dancing.

"What's happened? What's going on?" Senator Matthews ran to join the group as they rounded the building.

"We're not sure," Alice told him, noticing he had a long, jagged scratch on his left cheek, and a line of blood that was starting to clot. "Senator Matthews, you have a pretty bad cut there on your cheek."

He reached up and touched his cheek, then looked at the blood on his hand.

Nan walked up behind him, bundled in her husband's designer jacket. "We thought we heard screams," she said.

Shortly behind her, Sadie caught up with the group, her eyes red and puffy, as though she'd either been crying or had had a sudden attack of hay fever—which was unlikely in the snow. "I heard them, too," she said, out of breath.

"Several people thought they saw something fall past the window," Alice explained, not wanting to alarm them until they knew for sure what—or who—it had been. "We're going to check it out."

Chad, who had come outside just behind Sadie, heard this and rushed past them in the direction the rest of the group had gone.

From up ahead, where the group had already rounded the side of the building, there was another scream, which sounded like Pearl Ann again. Alice forged ahead and caught up with Franny and Owen, clearing the corner just in time to see Zeb getting up from where he had been kneeling next to a motionless mass in the snow. When Zeb stepped away to talk quietly to Ben and Luke,

Alice got a better look. She rubbed her eyes and looked again.

She felt her stomach turn over as she recognized the body. It was Roz Fender. And she most definitely was dead.

Alice looked up into the darkness, above the bank of windows in the great room and there, in the blowing snow high above the spot where Roz lay, was the empty widow's walk.

CHAPTER 7

It took twice as long for the ambulance to arrive as it should have. The snow was getting thicker, both on the ground and in the air. But soon, red flashing lights could be seen moving slowly up the drive toward the lodge. Zeb, Luke, and Ben stood in the driveway, waving flashlights, and Chad had turned on every one of the lodge's exterior lights. The ambulance pulled in, and two paramedics, along with Officer Dewey—another member of Blue Valley's tiny police department—jumped out.

"Good, Dewey. Glad you're here," said Ben, patting his colleague on the back.

"Sure thing, captain," said Dewey with a grin. "I was home watching TV, eating way too many cheese puffs, so this is actually a much better way to spend New Year's Eve."

As the paramedics, stretcher in hand, and Officer Dewey followed Luke and Ben, Alice heard them talking about the almost impassible road conditions.

"We were lucky we made it," one of their voices carried on the wind.

"This is awful!" Franny said, as she, Owen, and Alice huddled together at a distance.

"Owen, maybe you should take some pictures," said Alice.

"Seriously?" Owen looked at Alice, shocked.

"I mean, in case there are any clues that could be missed," said Alice.

"Or get covered with snow," added Franny.

"Oh. Good idea!" Owen began snapping shots of the scene, the crowd—everything and anything he thought might be relevant to the investigation.

The three of them moved a bit closer to where Zeb was talking to the paramedics. "Looks to me like she was pushed from that widow's walk up there," Zeb said, pointing up. "Died on impact. But we'll see. I'll head back into town with you guys."

Within a few minutes, Luke, Ben, and Dewey had marked off the scene using folding chairs that Chad and Sadie brought out along with the yellow tape Dewey had grabbed on his way over, and the paramedics and Zeb had loaded Roz's body into the ambulance and were pulling slowly down the drive.

"We're going to need everyone to gather in the great room," Luke announced to the few guests who were still out braving the cold.

Alice noticed that the senator and his wife had never gone back inside, but were standing by themselves, looking somber. Sadie was saying comforting words to Chad, who looked like he was still in complete shock. Everyone filed quietly back into the lodge and found seats in the great room, the festive mood from less than an hour before gone without a trace.

"We're going to need to talk to each one of you," Ben told the group. "So, if you could all just stay—"

Just then, the doors in the entryway flew open, and a chill wind blew a flurry of snowflakes inside.

"It's just us," Zeb said, leading the two paramedics into the room.

"We couldn't get through," one of the paramedics said. "The roads are impassable. No one's getting into or out of this place tonight."

Next to Alice, Owen gasped loudly.

"What?" Alice asked, turning to her friend.

"No one can get in or out," whispered Owen with a gulp.

"Well, there are worse places to be trapped," said Franny, leaning back into the plush sofa.

But as Owen looked at Alice, she realized what he was thinking. "No one can get in or out," she repeated. "That means the killer is someone in this room."

CHAPTER 8

"I'll get to the front desk," a weary Chad told the group. "If you'll come in a few at a time, I'll set you up in a room for the night." He turned to Sadie and Michael, who were standing nearby. "Sadie, take the master key and go check that the second-floor rooms are stocked. Michael, go tell Chef Louis what's happening, and tell him to prepare for a larger breakfast selection than he'd previously planned."

"Can we help?" Alice quickly asked, after Michael and Sadie were dispatched.

Chad looked relieved. "That would be great. Thank you. Come with me."

As he led Alice, Franny, and Owen to the front desk

area, just off the entryway, Owen tugged Alice's arm. "What are you up to?" he whispered.

"We need to help with the investigation," Alice answered. "And, I hate to say it, because I like the guy, but Chad is suspect *numero uno*."

Alice, Owen, and Franny weren't new to the mystery game. They'd helped the police solve several cases—even though the police, namely Ben and Luke, officially discouraged their involvement. But they got involved, anyway. Maybe it was because the three friends were naturally curious. Maybe it was because all three of them—being in the customer service business themselves—were good at reading people and formulating the right questions. But whatever drew them into the process of investigation, with each new case they solved, they seemed to be addicted to the excitement of the quest for the truth. And frankly, Blue Valley was better off because of it.

"You're right", whispered Franny. "Chad was upset with Roz because she was leaving him and possibly ruining him financially."

"He's worked so hard to get this place up and running, and clearly, has spared no expense," Alice agreed. "This is his dream. To be threatened with losing it all now would be, well—"

"Motive for murder?" Owen finished.

By that time, they'd arrived at the front desk area. Chad came out of the office holding the party guest list. "Let's see . . . I think we can accommodate everyone on the second floor. Adam and Nan were already booked, of course. They're up on the third . . ."

"You can put the three of us together," said Franny. "Ben told me he and Luke are going to stay downstairs to question everyone and stand guard."

"Great. I'll put you in 203 and 204." Chad swiped a set of key cards and handed them over. Then, he began running down the list of party attendees and assigning them rooms, occasionally asking who went with whom, so that he could put family members and close friends near one another.

Alice, Owen, and Franny delivered the keys to the guests, and returned to the front desk, where Michael was busily tapping away on the computer, and Chad, who appeared to have zoned out a bit, was standing and staring toward the windows on the opposite wall.

"You okay, Chad?" Alice asked quietly.

That snapped him out of his reverie. "What? Oh. I . . . don't know."

"We're so sorry for your loss," said Franny.

"My—oh. Thanks. It's still sinking in, I guess."

"We can help you tonight. I mean, there will be lots to do with so many unexpected overnight guests," Alice said. "Please, let us know if we can make things easier."

"Thanks, that, uh, means a lot." Chad looked down and shook his head, a sad smile on his face. "I still can't believe she's dead."

"You must be in shock," said Owen. He paused. "Chad, can you think of anyone here who would want Roz dead?"

"I keep hoping it was just an accident," said Chad. "But I heard the coroner say she was pushed. I mean, so I guess . . . I guess, it wasn't an accident. But who would kill her?"

"Well, don't worry. Detective Evans and Captain Maguire are on the case," said Owen. "They'll get to the bottom of this. And since we're all trapped here, at least the killer can't escape."

At this, Chad went a little pale. "Oh. I hadn't thought about that," he said, and swallowed hard. "If only I'd been there. I could've protected her. I could've . . ."

"You couldn't have known she was in danger," said Alice, reaching across the counter and patting him on the shoulder.

"And now—on opening night—there's a murderer under our roof!" Chad rested his elbows on the desk and buried his face in his hands.

"Like Owen said, the police will solve this thing," Alice assured him. "They'll start questioning each person any minute now." She gave a quick sideways glance at Owen and Franny. "They'll probably start by asking us where we were when Roz was pushed from the widow's walk. Glad we were all together in the great room," she said, motioning toward Owen and Franny.

Now Chad turned as white as a ghost. "I was—I was in my office," he said defensively, almost as though he'd just been accused of the crime. He pointed a thumb to the office door over his shoulder. "On the phone. With my supplier."

"At midnight on New Year's Eve?" Owen blurted out, then paused awkwardly. "Sorry."

"It was an emergency," Chad said defensively. "They shorted me on linens. Sheets and towels. People in this business keep crazy hours. Our busiest times are holidays and weekends, and . . . off-hours. That's when we get things done. I was lucky to catch him, actually." Chad cleared his throat. "Excuse me. I'm going to check on the guests." With that, he left the room.

"I hope that thing he said about the shortage of towels isn't true," said Owen. "I need extra for my bedtime ritual."

"Your bedtime ritual?" asked Alice, rolling her eyes at Owen.

"That's right. There's my hot bubble bath, then my cool shower, then my deep conditioning treatment, then I rinse. Oh—I might also need an extra one of those tiny bottles of conditioner."

Alice raised a brow at Owen.

"What? It helps me sleep. This hair takes a lot of maintenance!" he said, pointing at his thick, dark hair—which, admittedly, did always look perfect. He moved down the counter to where Michael was still working on the computer.

"Extra towels, Mr. James?" Michael asked as Owen approached.

"Why, yes, that would be wonderful."

Michael disappeared into the office and reappeared with a stack of fresh, white towels and several tiny bottles of shampoo, conditioner, and moisturizer.

"Wow," said Owen. "You're the best concierge I've ever encountered!"

"Thank you, sir," said Michael with a studious nod.

"Are you sure this is okay?" asked Alice, sidling up alongside Owen. "I mean, what with the linen shortage?"

Michael gave Alice a knowing nod. "There will be no linen shortage on my watch, Ms. Maguire."

"Oh. But I thought Chad said—"

"Mr. Fender did say there was a shortage." Michael

looked around, and when he saw that they were alone, leaned over the counter a bit. "Are you going to solve this case?" he whispered, his professional concierge façade falling away.

"What do you mean?" Alice said, surprised.

"I've read about you three in the paper," said Michael. "I know all about how you've helped the police solve murders. I can't believe you're here! It's an honor to meet you. You're local celebrities—and I'm a big fan!"

Jane Elkin had run an article about the three amateur sleuths in the *Blue Valley Post* back in the fall.

"Are you saying that there is no shortage of sheets and towels at the lodge?" asked Alice.

"I am a concierge," said Michael. "While I am loyal to this lodge and to my employer, I have not been paid to lie." He straightened his tie. "There is no shortage. I cannot imagine why Mr. Fender said there was, although, I'm sure he had his reasons."

"Wow! Thanks, Michael. And, thanks for the towels, too," Owen said.

"If you need further assistance, do not hesitate to let me know."

"Thanks!" said Franny.

"Well, we'd better go up to our rooms," said Alice, herding Owen and Franny in the direction of the great room. "But we'll be back down shortly. Meanwhile, you call us if you need anything at all. Okay, Michael?"

Michael gave them a little salute, and Alice, Owen, and Franny hurried through the great room and up the stairs. From the railing on the second floor, they could look down into the room and see tired party-goers stoking the fire and settling onto couches, as Ben, Luke, and Dewey conferred near the entrance to the dining room.

Once inside their rooms, they opened the adjoining doors, creating one big space.

"This place is fantastic," said Owen, coming in and taking a seat on one of the queen-sized beds in Alice and Franny's room. "We should come back sometime when no one's been murdered."

"Agreed," said Alice.

"I'm starved," said Owen. "Let's go down and rummage through the kitchen."

"Here," said Franny, opening her bag. "I have granola bars, crackers, and chocolate-covered macadamia nuts."

"Your bag is a mini-bar!" said Owen. "It's like one of those Mary Poppins carpet bags! Do you have, like, a floor lamp in there?"

"How can you be hungry, Owen? We've just consumed a five-course meal, s'mores, *and* cake."

"You know my metabolism!" said Owen in his own defense.

"Actually, I'm hungry, too," said Franny, popping a chocolate-covered nut into her mouth.

"We need to add longer runs to our list of resolutions," said Alice, flopping back onto the bed. "By the way, I just texted Ben and Luke and told them about the argument I witnessed between Chad and Roz earlier. They said to let them know if we see or hear anything that might have any bearing on the case."

"You know what we should do?" said Owen excitedly. "Make one of those murder boards, like on TV. You know, a list of suspects and clues?"

"Where would we do that?" asked Alice, sitting up and looking around the room.

Owen looked around, too, his eyes settling on the large, full-length mirror that hung on the wall. "Too bad we don't have any of those dry-erase markers," he said. "Well, we can just use the notes app on my phone."

"Ha! Not necessary, my dear Watson," said Franny, digging through her bag and producing a pack of dry erase markers.

"You've got to be kidding me," said Owen.

"I used these for the board I set out on the sidewalk in front of Joe's at the Hometown Holidays Festival. I changed our specials every morning, you know."

"Franny, you're the best," said Alice, plucking one of the markers out of the package and going over to the mirror. "So. Number one, we have Chad." She neatly wrote Chad's name on the mirror. "I heard him actually say he wished his wife was dead. We know he had reason to kill her. Who else?"

They sat silently for a moment.

"I saw something when we were all out in the woods," Alice finally said. "I'm not sure if it was anything, but I'm pretty sure I saw Senator Matthews and Roz sort of going off together. It was during the candlelit hike, so it was dark and shadowy. The two of them went off the trail, and I'm almost positive I saw Roz trying to hold hands."

"Oh, I think it's pretty clear that Roz and Adam were involved in some scandalous way," said Owen. "Did you see the way she stared at him at dinner? Or the way they danced together? We already know they used to date."

"Think about it. If Roz was leaving Chad, maybe she was planning to run straight into the senator's arms!" said Franny.

"That would *not* be good for his career," said Owen. "His image is squeaky clean. Doting husband. Nature lover. If he and Roz were having an affair, he would most definitely not want that exposed."

Alice wrote a number two, with *Senator Adam Matthews* next to it.

"If the senator wanted to avoid a scandal, surely his wife did, too," said Alice, writing a number three, and *Nan Matthews* on the mirror.

"Right!" said Owen. "A woman scorned and such."

Alice stood back and looked at the list. "Anyone else?"

"There is someone else," said Owen. "And, I'm only saying this because I worked with Roz on the cakes. She was a real shrew. She could drive someone to murder if they had to put up with her for long enough."

"Sadie," said Alice, going back to the mirror and writing Sadie's name.

"Of course!" said Franny. "Roz was making her life a nightmare. We all heard the way she talked to Sadie earlier. I imagine that could eventually drive a person to blow their top."

"Heck, if I had to put up with that every day, I would've been tempted to push her off the roof. No doubt about it," said Owen.

"So, we have four viable suspects," said Alice. "The senator and his wife, Sadie, and Chad."

The phone on the nightstand rang. Owen answered. "Alice and Franny's suite," he sang. After a conversation that consisted of "Oh, okay," and "Of course," and "See you in a few," Owen hung up and turned to Alice and Franny. "Speak of the devil," he said. "That was suspect *numero uno*."

CHAPTER 9

Chad had called to ask for help. It seemed people were milling around restlessly in the great room as they awaited their turns to be questioned by the police, and Chad wanted to put together a snack and some kind of activity, like a game or movie, to make things as pleasant as possible.

"This is the perfect opportunity," said Alice after rinsing her face with a quick splash of cool water and brushing her hair with the hairbrush Franny produced from her bag. "All of our suspects in the same room!"

"What if they go to bed after their turn with the police?" asked Owen. "Then we can't keep an eye on them."

"I already thought of that," said Franny. "I know exactly what to do. I'm making the coffee."

"Don't tell me. Your red-eye, triple-strong elixir of energy?" said Alice as they locked up their rooms and walked toward the staircase.

"It's the most popular morning drink at Joe's," said Franny. "Trust me, there's no way anyone's going to sleep after drinking it."

"Make mine a double," said Owen with a yawn. "Ooh! I'll get out the leftover cake, too. That'll be worth staying up for."

Once the cake was cut and plated and the coffee was hot, the guests began wandering over to the serving table Chad had set up in the great room.

"Thanks for doing this," he said, taking two cups of Franny's coffee.

"Of course!" said Alice. "We're glad to help." She noticed Chad turning to walk over to Sadie with the coffee. "Uh, by the way—"

Chad turned back.

Alice lowered her voice a little. "I was wondering . . .

Sadie is so nice. *Such* a great person. Where will she go now?"

"What do you mean?" asked Chad, a frown creasing his forehead.

"Well, she was Roz's assistant, wasn't she?"

Owen nodded, catching onto Alice's line of questioning. "With Roz gone . . ." he said.

Chad looked struck. He glanced back over at Sadie. "It's such a crazy night, I hadn't even thought about . . ."

"The fact that she's technically now out of a job?" Owen finished for him.

"Yeah."

"If I were her, I'd probably move either to a place where I had family or a place where I could get another job," said Alice.

"I'd move to wherever home was," said Franny. "Where is Sadie from, anyway?"

"Huh?" Chad looked up and refocused. "Oh. New England. A little town on the coast." He looked over at Sadie again, who was talking to Granny

Maguire. "Man, I hope she doesn't move back there."

With that, he took the coffees and went to join Sadie.

"Ah-ha!" said Alice. "Did you hear that? New England coast!"

"I know exactly what you're thinking," said Owen. "This place."

"This place?" said Franny, yawning.

"Franny, you need to drink a cup of that coffee," said Owen. "I've never felt more awake!"

"As we were saying, this lodge is clearly influenced by the New England coast," said Alice. "The widow's walk. The style of the shingles. The steep-pitched roofline. The color choices. It's like an ingenious blend of Tennessee and Connecticut. Or Nantucket. Someplace like that. That's why the design is so unique."

"Sadie clearly said she had nothing to do with the design of this building," said Owen. "But I have a feeling she was lying. And now, Roz is getting a prestigious award for *this*." Owen waved his arms around.

"Roz *was* getting an award," said Alice.

"I don't know about Sadie, but if the senator over there announced that someone else was receiving an award for my work, I'd be pretty peeved," said Owen.

"Sadie is a grown woman—and a person who has studied architecture, and she's clearly intelligent," said Franny. "I still don't understand why she would work for Roz if she was being mistreated."

"I can answer that." Michael had materialized as if out of thin air and was standing just behind them.

"Wow," said Alice, catching her breath after being startled by his sudden appearance. "Where did you come from?"

"That's the thing about concierges," said Michael. "We're invisible until we're needed." He picked up a mug and Franny filled it with coffee. He took a swallow. "That's just what I needed," he said, savoring the hot liquid. "I feel better already."

"What were you saying about Sadie and why she stayed with Roz?" asked Franny.

"That was one of the many ugly conversations I overheard between those two," said Michael. "Sadie couldn't leave Roz, because if she did, Roz had threatened to give her a bad reference. She said Sadie would never be a successful architect without her stamp of approval. She told Sadie she had to stay and work with her for at least another year, or her reputation would be flushed down the toilet. I believe those were her exact words."

"Thank you for telling us this, Michael," said Alice.

Michael gave a quick salute. "I've always been very grateful that Mr. Fender gave me my orders—not Roz." He took his coffee and went back in the direction of the office.

"I'd sure like to get a peek inside that notebook Sadie always carries around," said Owen.

"She said she keeps all of her ideas in there," said Alice, nodding in agreement.

The three of them looked to where Sadie was sitting next to Chad on the couch. The two of them were laughing and smiling a lot, and Sadie's faithful little notebook was right by her side, as usual.

"I have an idea," said Owen. "I'll create a distraction, and you take a peek in the notebook."

"What kind of distraction?" asked Alice.

"Ye of little faith!" said Owen, in response to the obvious note of skepticism in Alice's voice. "Just be prepared. And make it quick."

"Okay," said Alice. "Ready, Franny?"

"Ready," said Franny.

The two of them watched as Owen sauntered across the room. Just as he passed Chad and Sadie, he screeched loudly and fell onto the floor.

"What—Owen! Are you okay?" Chad jumped up.

"The pain!" Owen wailed. "Oh! The pain!"

Everyone in the room turned around to look.

"Don't worry, folks," Owen told the onlookers. "It's my trick knee. Chad, if you and Sadie could help me up, and maybe help me walk upstairs to my room . . ."

Sadie and Chad didn't waste a moment in working together to lift Owen to his feet. When Sadie turned back toward the couch as if she would go back and pick up her notebook, Owen leaned more heavily on her and cried, "Oh, please, can we hurry? I need to get upstairs at once!"

"Of course!" said Sadie, abandoning the idea of turning back.

As she and Chad fumbled Owen toward the stairs, Alice and Franny slipped right onto the sofa they had vacated. Once the guests had returned to their conversations and books and board games, Alice casually picked up the notebook.

"Hmm, what's this?" she said innocently, in case anyone was listening. "Looks like someone left a notebook here. I wonder whose it is."

Then, she and Franny quickly opened the notebook and began flipping through the pages.

"Hurry!" whispered Franny, glancing up toward the second-floor railing.

"Oh, wow. Check this out!" Alice had the notebook open to a page marked "Granddaddy." Then she flipped further. Page after page detailed ideas and inspirations for the lodge, right down to the very room they were sitting in.

"Look at that rendering of the fireplace!" said Franny.

"And those windows, right there!" said Alice, pointing at the great bank of windows to their left.

"Ooh. Put it away! They're coming back!"

They quickly stood and went over to the fireplace, where they warmed their hands. The door to the dining room where Luke and Ben were holed up was closed, and Officer Dewey was standing by.

"Everything going okay in there?" Alice asked him.

"Seems to be," said Dewey. "But no big leads, as far as I know."

"Have they questioned Sadie Green yet?" Alice whispered.

"Nope. But she's up next." He took a swig of coffee with a jittery hand.

"Dewey, how many cups of coffee have you had?" Franny asked.

"This is my third. I can't seem to get enough of the stuff!"

Alice looked around and saw that the energy in the room had definitely changed since the crowd had partaken of Franny's coffee. People were buzzing. Suddenly, the usually quiet, mild-mannered Norman McKenzie stood up and said, "I know! Let's have a sing-along!" Even more bizarre than that, the rest of the room—including Alice's parents and Granny—cheered the idea.

"Everyone, go get freshened up and meet back here at the piano in half an hour!" someone called out above the excited chatter.

"Well, I'd say your coffee worked," said Alice. "No one's interested in going to bed."

"Chef Louis has a wonderful selection of dark roasted arabica beans," said Franny with a little grin. "I skewed the water-to-bean ratio . . . a *lot*."

"I'm feeling ready to take on the world, and I only had one cup," said Alice. "Well, we'd better go upstairs and check on our patient."

Franny nodded. "In light of what we just saw in that notebook, we may need to move Sadie up a few notches on the list of suspects."

CHAPTER 10

"So, we were right!" Owen said with a satisfied flourish of his dry erase marker as he put a star next to Sadie's name. "I had a feeling Sadie was the one who really deserved that award."

"Owen, you smell amazing," said Franny, sniffing the air around him.

"Bedtime ritual," Owen said with a wink. "I only wish I had my comfy pajamas."

"Seriously? You took a bubble bath, a shower, *and* deep-conditioned your hair in the few minutes you've been up here?"

"No. I only did the shower part. I'll do the rest later."

"Well, it's a good thing you had to put your clothes back on, because we're going to a sing-along," said Alice.

"Sounds like fun," said Owen. "I couldn't sleep even if I wanted to. I just wanted to be clean. Murder scenes have that effect on me."

Alice walked over to the bed. "We have half an hour to freshen up, so—Hold on! When did these mints get here?"

Owen and Franny both looked where Alice was looking. The beds had been neatly turned down and there were small chocolate mints on each pillow.

"Turndown service! This place is the best!" said Owen, running into his own room and returning with several of the mints in his hand.

"But this is horrible!" said Alice. "This means someone was in our room!"

All eyes then shifted to the makeshift murder board on the mirror. There was a long pause.

"Owen, how could you not have noticed this sooner?" asked Alice.

"It must've been done while I was in the shower," said Owen. "Anyway, it was probably Michael who did it. And he's on our side."

"But what if it was Chad? Or even Sadie?" Alice let out a long groan and flopped down onto the bed face-first.

"Try one of these delicious chocolate mints," said Owen, setting a piece of candy next to Alice's head. "You'll feel better."

"Owen, this is a disaster!" said Alice. But she did acquiesce and eat the chocolate.

There was a knock on the door. Franny hurried over and peered through the peephole, then flung open the door.

"Granny!"

"Thought I'd check in and see if you're coming down for the sing-along," Granny said with a smile.

"Absolutely," said Owen. "We were just talking about it."

Granny examined the mirror. "Looks like you were talking about more than that," she said, snapping her fingers. "I was hoping you three were on the job!" She took a step closer to the mirror. "Let's see . . . Four suspects, huh?"

"We've got plenty of motives," said Alice. "But no proof of anything yet."

"We need evidence," said Owen, sitting on the bed next to Alice.

Granny nodded thoughtfully. "What have your photos and videos turned up?" she asked.

"My—" Owen stopped and looked at Alice and Franny, then slapped himself on the forehead. "We haven't even looked at them yet! I took tons of photos of the crime scene!"

"Get out your camera and let's have a look, then," said Granny, making herself comfortable. "But I'm not interested in the photos of the crime scene. I'm more interested in the photos you took *before* the crime was committed. I'd bet that's where the clues lie."

Owen took out the camera and everyone gathered around him.

He scrolled through lots of photos of the cake, and

people eating the cake, and people exclaiming over the cake. Then, he came to the group shot he'd taken by the fireplace.

"I used my wide-angle lens for this one," he said. "Let's see . . . I took it at eleven fifteen. You can see the tree . . ." Owen panned across the photo. "There you all are, there's the beautiful staircase . . ."

"Hold it. Who's that going up the stairs?" asked Granny.

Owen zoomed in on the figure. "Oh, wow," he said. "It's Roz. That was when she went upstairs to her room. She said she'd had too much champagne."

"And, somehow, she ended up on the widow's walk above the third floor. Not in her room. Does anyone know where the Fenders' suite is?" asked Alice.

"Second floor," said Granny. "Down the hall, around the corner. That's where your parents' and my rooms are. There's a separate section, through a glass door, that's reserved for staff."

"What's that in Roz's hand?" asked Franny, leaning closer to the photo.

"That I recognize," said Owen, zooming in on the

item in Roz's hand. "That's fine Irish tweed—Senator Matthews' jacket."

"What would Roz be doing with the senator's jacket?" asked Granny.

"Good question," said Alice. "Go to the next picture, Owen."

Owen flipped to the next picture—another shot of the group of friends. He scanned the room again and came to the staircase once more, where another person was ascending the steps.

"That's Chad!" said Alice. "Looks like he's on his cell phone."

"Didn't he tell us he was stuck in his office when Roz died?" asked Owen. "He was on the phone with his linen supplier." He rolled his eyes. "I never did buy that story. And Michael said there was no shortage of sheets and towels."

"Chad's office is on the first floor, by the entry," said Alice.

Granny looked back at the murder board. "So, we know Roz went upstairs a bit before midnight, carrying the senator's jacket. We know her husband, Chad, followed shortly."

"We know he lied about that," added Franny.

"Any more pictures, Owen?" asked Granny.

"The next thing I took was a video of Alice and Franny talking about their resolutions."

Owen found the video. "This was at eleven thirty-five." He pressed the *play* arrow, and there were Alice and Franny, laughing, standing between the fireplace and the staircase, listing fun goals for the new year—things like learning to knit and jogging more often.

"Stop!" said Alice. "That's Senator Matthews! Going up the stairs. See?"

Sure enough, there was the senator, looking left and right, then going upstairs. A few frames later, Nan went up. Then, there was a to-do about the countdown and Owen was panning around the room, looking for both the Fenders and the Matthews.

"If I'd been watching what I was filming more carefully, I'd have known none of them were around," he said. "But they all slipped up the stairs so quietly."

"We're not done yet. There goes Sadie," said Alice, pointing to the camera, where the tiny figure of Sadie was going upstairs. "That must've been when she went up to look for someone to lead the countdown."

"Did she ever come back downstairs?" asked Granny.

"I don't remember," said Alice. "Mayor Abercrombie did the countdown, and then . . ."

"Then, we saw Roz fall past the windows," Granny finished for her.

Owen scrolled past the video to the snapshots he'd taken outside when everyone ran out to see what had happened. "These didn't turn out very well," he said, expanding the view of the people gathered outside. "But here's Sadie. She did come outside."

"I remember now!" said Alice. "She looked upset—like she'd been crying."

"That's right!" said Franny.

"And, I think . . . yes, here's Chad," said Owen. "And here's the senator and his wife." He looked closer. "How about that? She's wearing his jacket."

"The jacket Roz carried upstairs . . . just before she

died." Alice let out a long sigh, got up, and circled Nan's name on the murder board. "If she had that jacket, she must've gotten it from Roz, right?"

"It certainly seems probable," said Granny.

"I have so many questions," said Owen, laying his camera aside. "Like, why did Chad lie about where he was when Roz was killed?"

"And why did Sadie lie about designing the lodge?" asked Franny.

"And what was the nature of the senator's relationship with Roz?" asked Alice.

"And how did Nan feel about that relationship?" asked Granny with a knowing nod. When the others looked at her, she said, "Yes, I noticed it, too. For all Roz and the senator's acting like they were *just friends*, anyone could see there was something else going on between them."

"We know that, basically, any of these people could've killed Roz," said Owen, getting up and pacing back and forth in front of the mirror. "All of them had motive, and none of them were in the room when she was pushed."

Granny's cell phone rang. "There's Chester," she said, smiling. "He says everyone's downstairs. We'd better go!" She hopped up and headed out the door. "See you downstairs!" she called back.

"Man, I hope it was Michael who turned down the beds," said Owen as they locked up and walked down the hall. "Ooh, look!" He stopped and pointed toward the windows that looked out onto the grand second-floor balcony, where a couple could be seen in what appeared to be a steamy embrace. "There's someone who *seriously* needs to get a room!"

"Who is that?" whispered Alice.

"Alice, they're outside," said Owen. "They can't hear us. You don't have to whisper."

Franny grabbed Alice's arm. "It's Sadie! Sadie and Chad!" she whispered.

"You're kidding!" Owen also whispered. "So, they're a couple?"

"Oh, man," said Alice. "Maybe we're not hunting for a single murderer. Maybe we're hunting for two!"

CHAPTER 11

From the railing of the second-floor overlook, Alice, Franny, and Owen watched the group in the great room. Everyone had gathered around the upright piano that was angled into the corner across from the fireplace.

"This is like our rooftop garden at home," said Franny, patting the railing. "We can see everyone from here."

"Let's spot our suspects," said Owen in a low voice. "Although, we already know where Chad and Sadie are." He wiggled his eyebrows.

"I didn't know Pearl Ann could play the piano," said Franny.

The whole group, joined by the members of the Gothic Trolls—who were stuck at the lodge just like everyone else—had just launched into a rousing round of what sounded like "Wouldn't It Be Lovely."

"That's from *My Fair Lady*!" Owen gave a little gleeful yelp.

"Focus, Owen!" said Alice, who found her own feet starting to tap as well. "We can't let the show tunes get to us. Look. There's Nan, sitting on the couch." She nodded in the direction of Nan, who sat alone.

"I wonder where the senator is," said Franny.

"She looks pretty glum," said Alice. "Let's take her a piece of cake and see what we can find out."

They went downstairs, grabbed a generous slice and a fork, and joined Nan. By then, the group at the piano had begun singing "One Day More" from *Les Misérables*, and Alice knew they'd be lucky if Owen could keep from leaping up and breaking into both song and dance.

"Hi, Nan," said Alice. "We thought you looked like you could use a piece of cake."

Nan looked at the cake for a moment, then mechanically reached out and took it.

"Are you okay?" Franny asked, touching Nan's arm.

Nan let out a long sigh. "Not really," she finally said.

"Because of Roz?" Alice asked.

Nan nodded, her eyes filling with tears that she somehow managed not to spill. "She was . . . She was very dear to Adam and me."

"We're so sorry," said Franny. "Had you known her long?"

"Adam knew her longer than I did," said Nan. "They'd even dated, once upon a time. But I've known her our whole married life—so around six years, I guess." She looked up and spotted Chad and Sadie, coming down the stairs. "Poor Chad," she said sadly.

"Poor Chad, indeed," said Owen, raising a brow at the couple.

"Where is the senator now?" asked Alice.

"In with the police," said Nan. "I'm up next. I'm a little nervous about that."

"Don't be," said Franny. "The dark-haired officer with the glasses is my husband, Ben—he's also Alice's brother. Detective Evans is our good friend. They just want to figure out who killed Roz. I'm sure you'll do just fine."

Alice watched Nan's face as Franny spoke, looking for any kind of reaction, but Nan's quiet demeanor was not phased. "They're asking things like where everyone was when Roz was killed," Alice offered.

"Of course," said Nan, nodding.

"Most everyone was here in this room, which simplifies matters," said Alice.

"I wish I could say the same for Adam and me," said Nan. "Neither of us was here. But the good news is, we were together in our room. So, at least we can vouch for each other—although, I don't know if it'll count for much, since we're married." She noticed Adam coming out of the dining room door next to the fireplace, handed the untouched cake to Franny, and stood. Then, she walked across the room without a backward glance.

"She's so . . . dignified," said Franny through a mouthful of cake.

"Franny, isn't that your fourth slice tonight?" asked Owen.

"I'm tired! I always crave sweets when I'm tired, okay?" said Franny, who looked a little guilty, but not guilty enough to give up the cake.

"Look, there's Michael," said Alice, standing. "Let's go talk to him. We can make sure it was him who turned down our beds and see if he's noticed anything else."

"Good idea," said Owen pulling Franny to her feet. "C'mon, cake girl."

Michael, who was bustling about, scribbling something on his clipboard, stopped what he was doing when he saw them approach. "How's the investigation going?" he asked in a low voice.

"We're starting to make some headway," said Alice. "Oh, by the way, thanks for the turndown service and the mints. That was you who did that . . . right?"

"Don't worry. It was me," he said, glancing around and leaning in. "And, yes, I saw your suspect list. I won't breathe a word!" He held up three fingers as if to pledge his discretion.

"Thank you, Michael," said Owen.

"Looks like we're about to scratch two names off that list," said Alice.

"Oh, really?" asked Michael, clearly wanting to hear more.

"Nan Matthews just told us that she and her husband were in their room together when Roz was pushed off the widow's walk," said Alice.

Michael frowned, then slowly said, "No . . . they weren't."

Alice, Owen, and Franny all instinctively stepped closer to Michael, so that the four were now in something of a huddle.

"I did their turndown service around that time," said Michael.

"But, didn't you *just* do it? We didn't find—"

"Oh, I just turned down *your* beds," Michael quickly said, "because none of you were expected to be overnight guests of the lodge." He looked around again, checking that the coast was still clear. "Senator and Mrs. Matthews were booked in for the weekend. I pride myself on turning down the beds when our guests are away from their rooms, and I knew everyone would be downstairs ringing in the new year at midnight. The senator specifically told me that he and his wife have a tradition of celebrating with friends and counting down, then toasting with champagne. So, I knew they would be downstairs. I can unequivocally guarantee that no one was in the Matthews' room at midnight."

"So, they're lying, too," said Owen, looking over at the group around the piano, which now included the senator. "This group is nothing but a bunch of lying liars!"

"What about Sadie and Chad?" Alice asked quickly. "Were they in their rooms around that time, too?"

"That, I can't help you with," said Michael. "They're staff, so they don't receive turndown service."

"Of course," said Alice, nodding. "Thank you, Michael. You've been a big help."

"Glad to be of assistance," said Michael. "Good luck! Oh—and Franny, that coffee of yours is amazing! I could stay up all night! Wish I'd known you back in college!" He hurried off toward the office.

"Back to square one," said Franny, licking the last dollop of frosting from her fork. "What are we going to do now?"

"We're going to question Nan again," said Alice. "After all, we know that Roz went *upstairs* carrying the senator's jacket. We know that Nan came *downstairs* wearing it."

"That's right," said Owen. "That, coupled with the fact that Nan just straight-faced, flat-out lied to us isn't sitting right with me."

"Me, neither," said Alice.

There was a pause, and Alice and Owen looked back over to Franny, who had subtly managed to pick up another slice of cake from the table. "Oh!" She set it down quickly and cleared her throat. "Me, neither."

CHAPTER 12

Just a few minutes after Nan had gone bravely into the dining room to be questioned by the police, she came out again and, after giving her husband a kiss on the cheek over by the piano, reclaimed her spot on the couch near the fire.

"Did everything go okay with the police?" Alice said as she and Franny sat down on either side of Nan, while Owen poked at the fire and tossed on another log.

"Just fine," said Nan, who looked relieved. "You were right. They were very kind."

"Good," said Franny.

"By the way, I love that jacket," said Owen, pointing the poker he was holding in Nan's direction.

Nan looked down at the jacket and then wrapped it a bit closer around herself. "It's Adam's. I got chilled earlier, when we all ran outside, after—"

"Midnight?" asked Alice.

"Yes," said Nan. "This is Adam's favorite jacket."

"What do you think of Blue Valley?" asked Alice, changing the subject and trying to find a segue to what she really wanted to ask Nan. "I mean, apart from the . . . murder, um, aspect."

Nan smiled at Alice. "I love it. I'd like to come back here sometime. Maybe in the spring."

"I hope you'll drop by my bookstore in town. And the lodge is a wonderful place, isn't it?" Alice continued. "The service is outstanding. Michael, for instance. The concierge?"

Nan was listening to every word Alice was saying, but she looked a little confused. "Oh, yes. The staff have been lovely."

"That turndown service was a nice touch, wasn't it?"

Alice was sure she saw a shadow of doubt cross Nan's face. "Yes. Little details like that make one's stay really special."

Owen caught on to Alice's line of questioning and squeezed himself onto the couch between Franny and Nan. "What kind of candy did you and the senator get?"

"We, um . . ."

"I guess you probably saw Michael when he came in to turn down your bed," said Franny, leaning around Owen. "He said he made the rounds at midnight. He prides himself on being invisible."

"But, really, Michael's timing is a stroke of luck for you and the senator," said Alice. "That's another alibi for you both—I mean, not that anyone would ever think that either of you would harm Roz."

Now Nan was looking decidedly less calm.

Just then, Chad walked up to them. "Just checking around," he said. "Does everyone have everything they need? Are you all happy with your rooms?"

"Excuse me," said Nan, abruptly rising from the couch. "I'll be back shortly."

"Was it something I said?" asked Chad.

"No, I doubt it had anything to do with you," said Alice, watching Nan, who had joined her husband by the piano and was whispering in his ear.

"How are you holding up?" Franny asked, scooting closer to Owen so that Chad could take a seat.

Ben and Luke, along with Officer Dewey, joined them by the fireplace, then. Alice noticed that they all looked tired and was anxious to compare notes.

"I'm okay," said Chad. "Better."

"Good," said Alice.

"Oh, by the way," said Owen, "I had no problem getting a whole stack of extra towels."

Chad looked blankly at Owen. "Good?" he said slowly.

"I mean, because I know you were worried about the shortage and all."

A glimmer of understanding dawned in Chad's eyes. "Oh. Right. The, um . . ." Chad seemed to feel all six sets of eyes on him now, and he visibly deflated. "There was no shortage of linens," he finally said.

Luke took a step closer. "Would you like to clarify your earlier statement, Mr. Fender?"

Chad looked up at him, then at Ben and Dewey. "I think I'd better," he said. "I wasn't on the phone with my supplier. I was on the phone with my lawyer. And, I wasn't in my office. I was in my room. I lied because . . . well, it's a long story."

"We have all night," said Luke. Alice loved that she could see both compassion and firmness in his face.

Ben took out the little notebook he always kept in his breast pocket and uncapped his pen.

"Earlier today, before you all got here, Roz told me she was leaving me and taking half of everything, including this place. I called Andrew—that's my attorney. Andrew M. Shill." He paused as Ben wrote down the name. "What I didn't know was that Roz had already retained Andrew for her side of the divorce. We've used him for years, for everything. I'd left a message with him this afternoon, after Roz told me her plans. He finally called me back, believe it or not, just before midnight. I was fit to be tied. He's a slime ball, really. He offered to help me out, under the table, if I'd double his fee. That guy really ought to be disbarred. He even mentioned that I should pay him to rewrite my will, because if anything happened to me before the divorce was final, Roz would get everything. Then, he jokingly said that the same was true if anything happened to Roz—then, I would get everything, and my troubles would be over."

"Wow, he really is a slime ball," said Franny.

"Why didn't you tell us all of this in the first place?" asked Ben.

"I was afraid that if everyone knew about Roz's plan to leave me on Monday, and if Andrew ever mentioned that we'd literally just talked about what would happen in the event that Roz met with an untimely death, you'd see that as motive to kill her."

"Well, it *is* motive to kill her," said Luke. "But, Mr. Fender, we already knew about Mrs. Fender's plan to leave you." His eyes flicked to Alice for just a split second, then back to Chad.

"Chad, this also means you have an alibi," said Alice. "If you were talking to this Shill guy, and he can vouch for you—"

"Of course!" said Chad, brightening a little. "I've

been in shock basically all day—first, with Roz dropping that bomb on me, then with her dying like that . . . And I was so disgusted with Andrew that it didn't even occur to me that he could be an actual *help* to me."

"Mr. Fender, let's go back into the dining room. We'll take down a whole new statement and check in with this Andrew Shill," said Ben.

Just before heading into the study, Luke turned back and rejoined Alice, Owen, and Franny. "Good job," he whispered.

"You're not even going to get upset that we meddled?" asked Alice.

"Not this time," said Luke. "Let's all meet in half an hour. There's a little study, just the other side of the dining room. Meet us there and we can compare notes." He hurried off to catch up with Ben.

"So," said Owen with a satisfied smile. "We've finally hit the big time. The police want to compare notes with us."

"They've finally figured out they need us," added Alice.

There was a pause as Owen and Alice turned to Franny, who normally would've chimed in at that moment. But all they heard from Franny, who had apparently just conked out, was a loud snore.

"That's what four slices of cake will do to a person," said Alice, shaking her head.

"Simple carbs," Owen agreed.

"Let her sleep. We'll wake her in half an hour."

CHAPTER 13

The study, although a smaller room, was Alice's favorite. It boasted yet another stone fireplace, but this one was flanked on both sides by floor-to-ceiling bookshelves. More bookshelves lined the walls, covering every bit of space other than the French doors leading into the room and the windows along one wall which, in the daytime, overlooked a meadow with the Smoky Mountains beyond.

Alice and Owen had roused Franny, who seemed somewhat refreshed after her cake-induced slumber. The three of them found Ben and Luke waiting in the study.

"Chad was telling the truth," said Ben as they all settled into the comfortable reading chairs and plush sofa. "Dewey's processing his new statement, but we checked the phone record and double checked with Chad's attorney, Mr. Shill. Boy, that guy is a piece of work!"

"Andrew M. Shill, shifty attorney." Luke gave a little laugh. "He might be a jerk, but he was honest about the phone call with Chad. They hung up about five minutes after midnight. Looks like Chad is off the suspect list."

"Speaking of suspect lists, let's talk about what we know so far," said Alice.

"Yeah," said Owen. "Like, for example, what Nan and the senator told you about where they were when Roz died."

Ben cringed a little. "Just to be clear . . . I mean, on the record . . . this is an official police investigation. I don't want you three getting into the habit of nosing around in murder." He looked at his wife. "It's not safe."

"Uh, too late?" said Owen. "We hear about a crime, we automatically want to nose around."

"We can't help ourselves," said Alice.

"We should wear t-shirts that read 'Official Meddler' across the front," said Owen. He looked at Alice and Franny. "Who knew solving crimes could be so addictive? We're just a bunch of do-gooders."

"As I was saying," said Ben, raising an eyebrow at Owen. "We're all in a tricky situation here tonight, and—"

"And we aren't going to pretend you three haven't been hugely valuable to us in the past," Luke finished for him. "You have. So, even though, officially, we can't go around discussing matters such as this with civilians, we are going to . . . in light of this odd situation . . ."

"Swap notes with us?" Owen said.

"Uh. Yeah," said Ben.

"Let me guess," said Alice. "Both Senator Matthews and his wife claimed they were in their room, together, at midnight. Right?"

Ben and Luke looked at each other.

"Yes, that's correct," Ben said.

"Well, they weren't," said Franny.

"Are you sure?" asked Luke.

"Michael was turning down their beds and leaving those little mints on their pillows at midnight," said Owen.

"He saw no sign of them," added Alice.

"And look at this," said Owen, taking his camera strap off his neck and scrolling through the photos. "Here's the group photo I took tonight, and you can see Roz in the background, going upstairs, carrying the senator's snazzy jacket." He passed the camera to Luke who showed it to Ben.

"Okay," said Ben. "Are you positive that's the senator's jacket?"

"Seriously?" asked Owen. "Have you no fashion sense at all?"

"That's the same jacket that Nan is wearing right this very minute," said Alice.

"Look at the timestamp on the photo," said Owen.

"Eleven fifteen," said Luke.

"Just before Roz was murdered," said Alice.

"How did that jacket get from Roz's hands to Nan?" mused Owen.

"Nan said her husband gave it to her," said Franny. "When we all ran outside after Roz fell."

"Why would Roz take the senator's jacket in the first place?" Luke wondered.

"We suspect the two of them were involved . . . in an inappropriate way," said Franny.

"Alice saw them schmoozing it up in the woods," said Owen.

"Maybe she and Senator Matthews were going to meet—you know, in secret," said Alice. "Maybe they *did* meet, and he took his jacket back."

"And then shoved her off the roof," added Owen.

Ben was furiously making notes in his little notebook. "If they were having an affair, he wouldn't want that to go public."

"Right. But there's another suspect, too," said Alice.

"Sadie," said Franny. "Owen faked a trick knee so we could get a look at that notebook she's always carrying around, and guess what?"

"What?" asked Ben.

"She designed this place!" said Franny.

"And Roz was about to get an award for it," said Owen.

"And Roz treated Sadie horribly," added Alice.

"And we just saw Sadie and Chad in *flagrante*," said Owen, raising a brow.

"What?" said Luke.

"Yep. Out on the second-floor balcony. I'd give them a PG-13 rating."

"How's that for a big old cloud of suspicion over Sadie?" asked Alice.

Ben and Luke's cell phones buzzed in unison, and they both checked them.

"It's Zeb. He's examining the body out in the ambulance. He needs us to come out," said Luke, getting up. He looked back at Alice. "See if you can confront Sadie about her notebook. See if you can get her to crack. But stay together and around other people. I don't want you in danger."

With that, he and Ben hurried out of the room, and a moment later, Sadie came in.

"Hey, speak of the—" Owen started to say, but was stopped by a swift elbow in the ribs, courtesy of Alice.

"Oh, hello," said Sadie. "I was just—"

Alice had an idea. She stood up abruptly and rushed past Sadie in the direction that Luke had gone and sideswiped her right in the arm that held the leather notebook. And it worked. The notebook toppled to the floor.

"Oof!"

"Sorry!" Alice said, feeling a smidge of genuine guilt as she quickly bent down to pick up the notebook—just as Sadie was also bending down.

"Ouch!" Sadie said, as Alice's head accidentally collided with hers.

"Oh! Sorry again!" said Alice, flipping the notebook open as she handed it back to Sadie and looking at one of the many pages devoted to the lodge with faux shock. "Wait—what's this?" She looked up at Sadie.

Owen took the opportunity to show off his acting skills. "Am I—I mean, isn't that—I'm sorry, but that looks like the great room in this lodge!" He pointed at the sketch. "Sadie, *you* designed this lodge! Not Roz!"

Sadie looked, wide-eyed, at the sketch, then turned bright red. "Those are just studies . . . Of Roz's design," she stammered.

"Sadie," said Franny quietly. "Roz is no longer here to berate you, or bully you, or shrink you down to the size of a pin."

Tears sprang to Sadie's eyes.

"This place—*your* design—is spectacular," said Alice. "You're an amazing architect!"

Sadie sniffled and sat down on the couch. She chuckled through her tears. "Roz helped. Not very much, but a little bit."

Alice, Owen, and Franny sat down with Sadie.

"Tell us why a brilliant young woman stayed with a horrible employer for so long. Was it just because Roz would have blackballed you out in the architecture world?"

Sadie wiped the tears from her cheeks. "I was afraid of her—afraid of what she might be able to do to my reputation. But there are a couple of other reasons. The first was that Roz kept promising I'd get to work on bigger projects—that she would let me fly solo. I know it's stupid, but I believed her. Now, I can see it was all a manipulation because she didn't want to lose me."

"What was the second reason?" Franny gently prompted.

Sadie looked down at her hands. "In light of Roz's death, this is going to sound really sleazy. But I was —I *am*—in love with Chad. Have been since I met him five years ago." She sighed. "And, of course, put this all together, and who do you think killed Roz?"

There was a pause.

"So, you didn't kill Roz?" Alice asked.

"No. I did not."

"Then, where were you tonight at midnight when Roz was pushed?" asked Owen.

"In my room," Sadie said, sounding defeated. "Crying my eyes out. I went there because I didn't want to be in the great room at midnight and have to watch Roz kiss Chad like she does every year."

"Didn't you know she was leaving Chad?" asked Franny.

"Not until Chad told me a while ago, when we went off by ourselves for a few minutes."

"Where did you go off by yourselves?" asked Owen.

"The second-floor balcony," Sadie said, reaching for a tissue from the box on the end table. "I'm awful. I was happy to hear their marriage was ending. And Roz is dead!" She blew her nose loudly. "What kind of a person have I become? I've never been able to tell Chad how I felt, and when he told me the news, I —I hugged the stuffing out of him. I feel like a complete idiot."

Alice, Owen, and Franny exchanged subtle nods.

"Sadie, I want you to think about this next question," said Alice. "Is there *any* way you can think of that you could prove you were in your own room when Roz was killed?"

"Did anyone see you going in or coming out?" Franny asked.

Sadie thought for a moment. "No. I mean, I was just up there, writing in my diary like a twelve-year-old." She paused. "Wait. I keep my diary on my tablet computer. It's digital. It would've recorded the time!" She jumped up from the couch and started toward the study door. "Come with me. I'll show you."

They jogged behind Sadie as she hurried up the stairs and down the hall to the staff apartments. She unlocked her door and they all went inside.

"Look. See?"

She held out the journal entry from earlier that evening.

"Dear Diary . . ." Owen began reading aloud.

"Owen!" said Alice and Franny at once.

"We will respect your privacy and not read the entry," said Alice through clenched teeth, giving Owen a look.

"But look!" said Owen, pointing at the top right-hand corner of the screen where the date and time had been recorded. "You really were writing when Roz was killed."

Sadie breathed a sigh of relief.

"Take this straight to Captain Maguire, Detective Evans, or Officer Dewey," said Alice. "It might not be definitive proof, but—"

"I almost forgot!" said Sadie. "This tablet has a built-in GPS. They can see that I was in this room when I wrote this entry. It'll prove I'm telling the truth! And I can even come clean about my troubles with Roz now. I was so afraid that if I was honest about all that, everyone would assume I killed her." She looked at the three of them. "I feel like I've just been set free! Thank you so much!"

Sadie showed them out of her room but left them in the hall as she rushed off to find Luke, Ben, or Dewey.

"So, Sadie didn't do it," said Alice as they watched her go.

"And Chad didn't do it," said Franny.

"That leaves the Matthews," said Owen. "Are we betting on the wayward senator or the dutiful wife?"

CHAPTER 14

As they followed the hallway back across the second floor, Alice spotted a lone figure, shrouded in shadow, standing out on the balcony.

"Hold on. Is that—" She walked over to the glass doors, then looked back at Franny and Owen. "It is!"

"It is *who*?" asked Owen.

"The senator!" whispered Alice.

"Again, with the whispering," said Owen. "Alice, he's outside."

"Let's go," said Alice, and she pushed open the door and stepped out into the icy air.

The senator turned to see who'd come outside, then turned back to look at the starry sky. "Looks like the snow finally stopped," he said quietly.

"Wow, the sky cleared up," said Owen. "There must be a million stars out."

The senator nodded silently, and they all came to stand beside him to marvel at the sky.

"I learned a lot of these constellations when I created the cake," said Owen. "There's Orion, I think."

"Any idea which one is Hercules?" asked the senator, and now, Alice could hear a touch of a slur in his voice. Her eyes automatically went to the drink in his hand, which looked like scotch.

"I believe Hercules is a summer constellation, Senator Matthews," she said.

"Please, call me Adam." He took a drink. "Just plain Adam."

"Sen—Adam, if I may," said Owen. "What made you ask about Hercules in particular? I mean . . . Is it your favorite constellation?"

Alice gave Owen a pointed look, and Owen shrugged his shoulders.

"Long story," said Adam. "Used to be my nickname." He took another big swig of scotch.

"Hercules? Wow. Someone must've been pretty crazy about you, to call you that," said Franny.

Adam didn't comment. He just chuckled to himself.

"We talked to your wife earlier," Alice said. "She was really broken up about Roz's death. We didn't realize you were so close to Roz. Sorry for your loss."

Adam drank down the rest of his drink, then dumped the ice cubes over the railing and watched them fall to the snowy ground below.

"That's a great bracelet you're wearing," said Franny. "I like that symbol. What does it mean?" Franny gave Alice and Owen a wide-eyed look behind the senator's back.

"That?" He looked at the bracelet and tried to focus. "That little swirly thing . . ."

"The triskele," Alice said softly.

"What does it mean?" Franny asked Adam.

"I don't know what it's supposed to mean," he said. "To me, it means past, present, and future." His voice cracked on the last word. "Sorry." He cleared his throat. "A dear friend gave me this." He took off the bracelet and handed it to Franny.

"Senator—"

"It's Adam." His face clouded over. "Just Adam."

"Sorry, I—" Franny started to hand the bracelet back to him, but he held up a hand.

"No. You keep it. I don't want it." He burped loudly. "Now, it doesn't even matter." He whirled around and looked at Owen. "Did I tell you that was the best cake I've ever tasted?"

"What? You actually ate a piece?"

"Yes. It was outstanding." He hiccupped. "And, it had Hercules on it. Roz showed me."

"Yes, it did," said Owen. "She specifically requested that. And thank you, Adam." Owen pointed at the camera which was hanging from the strap around his neck. "I wonder, would you mind coming downstairs and letting me take your picture eating the—"

"Owen!" Alice stepped in front of him. "Can't you see that Adam is upset? Now is not the time for cake."

"No, no, no," Adam mumbled. "It's okay. But I can't do the cake right now because I have to go talk to the police."

"You do?" asked Alice.

"Yes, I do," Adam affirmed, now tossing his glass over the balcony railing and stumbling toward the door.

"Can we help you?" asked Franny.

"No, I need to go by myself." With that, Adam shoved open the door and walked hurriedly toward the staircase.

"We should follow him," said Owen.

"Hold on. I just got a text from Luke," said Alice. "He's asking where we are." She tapped their location into the phone, and it quickly dinged again. "He says to stay right here."

"What's going on?" Franny asked, looking worried.

Before anyone could take a guess, the balcony door

swung open and Ben and Luke came out.

"Have you seen Senator Matthews?" asked Ben.

"Yes. He was just here. He went to find you," said Alice. "Didn't you pass him?"

"Which way did he go?" asked Ben.

When Alice pointed, Ben rushed off in that direction.

"Luke, we need to talk to you about the conversation we just had with Adam—Senator Matthews," said Alice. "All signs point to the fact that he was much more involved with Roz than he should've been."

"Yeah, there was the Hercules thing, and the Triscuit thing," Owen said.

"*Triskele*," Alice corrected. "He seemed to be very drunk, and—"

Luke raised a hand. "I want to hear all of this, Alice, but right now, I need you all to go to your room and wait for us there."

"What?" Alice felt her heart go into high gear.

"Zeb called us out to the ambulance. They're still stuck here, but, meanwhile, he's been examining the body. He found something, under Roz's fingernails. Of course, it's inconclusive until we can take some real samples and have them analyzed, but when Zeb checked the fingernails, he found—well, let's just say that it would appear Roz took a swipe at her attacker."

A light dawned in Alice's eyes. "The scratch! On the senator's face!"

"Yes. I've got to go. Wait for us in your room." He shoved the door open and ran in the same direction Ben had gone.

Alice, Owen, and Franny looked at each other for a split second, then took off all at once for their room, running into one another as they tried to squeeze through the door together.

"Now what do we do?" Franny said, pacing the room once they were safely inside.

"We wait. And pray that Ben and Luke are safe," said Alice.

Her phone dinged.

"It's Luke. The senator is nowhere to be found. They think he's making a run for it." Alice swallowed hard. "He says to lock our door."

CHAPTER 15

The room was too quiet. Alice felt as though the snow outside had covered everything and muffled all sound.

"This is the worst," Owen finally said. "Just sitting here. Not knowing what's happening." He peered out the window into the darkness.

"Can you see anything?" Franny asked, joining him at the window.

"Nothing," said Owen.

"Wait. Listen," said Alice. She went to the door and peeked through the peephole.

"See anything?" asked Owen.

"No, but I hear something." Alice paused.

"I hear it, too," said Franny, coming to the door. "Someone's crying!"

Alice opened the door a crack and saw Nan, sitting on the floor in the hallway, softly crying.

"Nan! Are you okay?" she asked.

"No," said Nan, sniffling. "My husband—I think he . . ." She reached into the pocket of the senator's jacket, which she still wore. "I found this in his pocket." She held out a shimmering diamond triskele on a fine gold chain.

"Roz's necklace!" said Franny.

Nan began to sob. "That's right. *Roz's* necklace." She got to her feet, stumbling a little. Alice hurried over to help her stand. "Don't you see what this means? Adam must have—" She looked at Alice. "My husband must be a murderer. I'm so frightened!"

"Nan, come inside," said Alice, looking up and down the hall, feeling a shiver run down her spine. "It might not be safe out here. Let's talk about it. It's going to be okay."

Nan nodded and followed Alice into the room, where Owen invited her to sit, and Franny handed her a box of tissues.

"He killed her! He must have! It all makes sense now. I feel like such a fool," said Nan, wiping her eyes, then raising them and catching sight of the mirror. "What . . ." She squinted at the list of names, her eyes seeming to rest on her own name, which was circled several times.

"Oh!" Owen jumped up and stood in front of the mirror. "Pay no attention to this!"

"We were just trying to help," said Alice. "Please know that we never thought you killed Roz. We were just thinking out loud . . . on the mirror."

"I understand. It's okay." Nan looked down, a deep crease forming between her brows. "I still can't believe Adam did this," she said, her voice sounding colder now.

"Any idea why?" asked Owen.

"Because they were having an affair," said Nan matter-of-factly.

"*You knew?*" asked Alice.

Alice's phone dinged and she glanced at it. It was Luke, saying they'd found the senator. Face-down in the snow . . . beneath the widow's walk.

"They found—" Alice's heart jumped into her throat. When she looked back up, she saw Nan watching her closely. Every nerve in Alice's body stood on-edge.

"Who was that?" asked Nan.

"Nobody," said Alice quickly. "Just my mother."

"Give me the phone."

"What?" asked Alice.

In one swift movement, Nan snatched Alice's phone from her hand and read Luke's message. She looked back at Alice and silently slid a meat cleaver out of her purse. "You really should learn to hide your emotions better, Alice. You've figured it out. I can see that." She scoffed. "I'm so sick of people who want to ruin everything." She moved her eyes from Alice, to Owen, to Franny.

"You have a . . . giant knife," said Owen, aghast.

"So, you, uh, knew all about the affair?" asked Franny with a gulp.

. . .

"Of course, I knew. I've had to know for all these years. I've had to live in the shadow of that woman since day one."

Alice attempted to calm Nan. "You've been so patient. Such a faithful—"

"I've been an idiot!" Nan blurted out. "And tonight, when that little minx lured Adam up to the widow's walk, so she could kiss him at midnight instead of me, his wife—well, I couldn't let her get away with it." She waved the cleaver angrily. "After everything we've worked for. All the good we've done! All of it would've meant nothing if the public found out about my husband's indiscretions! All anyone would remember us for would be the scandal!"

Owen's eyes were huge as he looked from Alice to Franny.

Franny took a small step forward. "Mrs. Matthews—"

"Not another word!" Nan lunged at Franny, cleaver in hand.

Alice had never seen Owen fly through the air, but, somehow, he did at that moment.

"No! She's pregnant!" he yelled, landing between Franny and Nan.

The cleaver glanced off Owen's left shoulder and clattered to the floor. Franny quickly stepped on it, and Alice grabbed Nan from behind, pinning her arms. Owen joined her, and Franny ran to the door, flung it open, and screamed for help. Within moments, Ben and Luke were in the room, and once they'd made sure everyone was okay, they took Nan away.

Alice, Owen, and Franny sat down on the bed, still in shock.

The room was quiet for a full two minutes before Bea, Martin, and Granny rushed in. There was much checking on everyone and hugging and chatter about what had happened. As Alice's mother wrapped her into a tight hug, Alice met Franny's eyes over Bea's shoulder. Owen's words had just sunk in.

Alice's eyes filled with happy tears. So did Franny's.

CHAPTER 16

The sunrise over the Smokies was something to behold. It lit up the sky and made the snow-covered landscape shimmer with unimaginable brilliance.

The whole Maguire family—including their "adopted" son Owen, along with Luke and Chester emerged from the lodge onto the grand second-floor balcony after a delicious breakfast.

The ambulance had finally made its way back into town, and Nan Matthews had been taken into custody. Senator Matthews had been very lucky to survive the fall from the widow's walk, in part due to his relaxed state of drunkenness, and it part due to the fact that he'd landed in a thick snowdrift—and thus had been able to tell the police that Nan, after begging him to come up and talk things out with her, had told him how she'd killed Roz and that he would have to suffer the same fate.

Once Nan had seen that there was no escape, she'd made a full confession. The saddest irony was that—whatever lingering feelings of love and regret Adam had toward Roz—he'd never actually had an affair with her. Roz had invited him up to the widow's walk for a midnight kiss, and he'd refused her, which made her angry enough to take a swing at him, scratching his face in the process. But Nan hadn't known that.

Meanwhile, Sadie had agreed, on Chad's invitation, to stay in Blue Valley and work with him to create the next phases of the lodge. The last Alice had seen of the two of them, they were having breakfast in the kitchen with Chef Louis and Michael, all of them discussing their plans for the future.

Alice's hand was warm tucked into Luke's, even in the cold morning air, and although she was exhausted, she felt a wonderful surge of invigoration. It was the first day of a whole new year, after all. There would be a brand new round of cozy evenings at Luke's cabin, fun mornings in the rooftop garden, walks in the park and by the lake, and festivals, and fairs, and friends. And, there would be family.

"So, it's true, then?" Alice looked from Ben to Franny.

Ben beamed with pride and cleared his throat. "I guess we have an announcement to make," he said. "Just a very small announcement."

Bea put a hand to her chest. "Go ahead," she said.

Ben looked at a smiling Franny and said, "We're expecting the next little Maguire to arrive this summer!"

"It's early yet," said Franny. "We were going to tell you once I was through the first trimester, but Owen figured it out." She turned to Owen. "How on earth did you know?"

"I didn't even *know* I knew until Nan came at you with that cleaver!" said Owen. "But I guess it all added up: the mints, the crackers, the four pieces of cake . . . You never drank wine or champagne. You were tired. I think in that moment, I just . . . put it together."

The whole group broke into joyous congratulations

and hugs, and Alice even caught sight of Bea doing a little jig with Owen, and singing, "I'm going to be a grandmother!"

"I'm going to be a *great*-grandmother!" said Granny.

"The most beautiful great-grandmother the world has ever seen," said Chester, taking Granny's hand. "And since we're all together, as a family, I mean . . . I mean, I've been planning to ask, and now seems like the time." Chester got down on one knee, and a collective gasp went up from the group. He looked up at Granny. "Georgie?" He cleared his throat and started again. "Georgina Maguire, you and I have been friends since I can remember. I think I've loved you forever. Today is the beginning of a new year, and I want to spend every single day of it . . ." He paused and smiled into Granny's eyes. "With you."

"Well, Chester, I—"

"Now hold on. Let me finish. I want to spend every day of *every* year with you. Georgie, will you marry me?"

Granny's eyes filled with tears, and she put her hands on her cheeks, her face breaking into a huge smile. "Yes, Chester. I will gladly marry you!"

Alice's heart felt like it would burst. "If this is any indication of the kind of year we're about to have, I can't wait!"

Everyone gathered around Franny and Ben, and Granny and Chester. But Luke pulled Alice to one side of the group. "I can wait," he said softly into her ear.

She met his eyes and knew exactly what he meant. This was Franny and Ben's moment, and this was Granny and Chester's moment. A year's worth of moments even more wonderful than this one was in store.

She pulled Luke close. "I can wait, too," she said, and kissed him. "That's the kiss we missed at midnight."

"Happy New Year, my Alice," Luke said, leaning in and stealing another kiss.

"This calls for a song," Owen announced. "Since I missed all the showtunes last night, how about a round of that song everyone always sings at the start of a new year?"

At that, the whole family launched into the song.

"Should old acquaintance be forgot . . ."

Owen walked over and put his arms around Alice and Franny. "You know, it's just occurred to me that I don't really know the words to this song," he said. "And I don't even know what *old angzine* means."

Both Owen and Franny automatically looked at Alice.

"What? You think I know everything?"

Owen and Franny kept looking at Alice.

"Okay, okay." She sighed. "The song is actually a poem, written in Scots by Robert Burns. *Auld lang syne* means times long past. It's about remembering old times and old friends." She smiled at them. "It's about taking to heart what a blessing they are."

"Done," said Owen, giving Alice and Franny a squeeze that turned into one big hug.

Alice smiled at her friends, feeling a wonderful mixture of joy and peace. "This is going to be our best year yet."

AUTHOR'S NOTE

I'd love to hear your thoughts on my books, the storylines, and anything else that you'd like to comment on —reader feedback is very important to me. My contact information, along with some other helpful links, is listed on the next page. If you'd like to be on my list of "folks to contact" with updates, release and sales notifications, etc.… just shoot me an email and let me know. Thanks for reading!

Also…

… if you're looking for more great reads, Summer Prescott Books publishes several popular series by outstanding Cozy Mystery authors.

CONTACT SUMMER PRESCOTT BOOKS PUBLISHING

Twitter: @summerprescott1

Bookbub: https://www.bookbub.com/authors/summer-prescott

Blog and Book Catalog: http://summerprescottbooks.com

Email: summer.prescott.cozies@gmail.com

YouTube: https://www.youtube.com/channel/UCngKNUkDdWuQ5k7-Vkfrp6A

And…be sure to check out the Summer Prescott Cozy Mysteries fan page and Summer Prescott Books Publishing Page on Facebook – let's be friends!

CONTACT SUMMER PRESCOTT BOOKS PUBLISHING

To download a free book, and sign up for our fun and exciting newsletter, which will give you opportunities to win prizes and swag, enter contests, and be the first to know about New Releases, click here: http://summerprescottbooks.com